A GOOD DAY TO DIE

As soon as the Penetrator's eyes wavered, Benny struck, thrusting with the billy toward the outer edge of Mark's thigh. The tip burrowed between the layers of muscle, stretching the skin ahead of it, barely missing the bone. Tissue ruptured and nerve trunks ceased to transmit their messages. The pain was astounding. Signals of blinding agony were going to the brain.

Then Benny moved in for an overhead attack, intent on bloodying his opponent's head, battering him into unconsciousness with the lead-loaded club. Mark brushed the attack aside with his left forearm, thrusting his right foot into the man's stomach. Pivoting through the air over Mark's head, Benny landed on the tile-covered cement floor like a sack of wet manure. Air burst from his mouth, and he lay still . . .

The Penetrator Series

THE
PENETRATOR

MARDI GRAS MASSACRE

by
Lionel Derrick

PINNACLE BOOKS • NEW YORK CITY

THE PENETRATOR: MARDI GRAS MASSACRE

An original Pinnacle Books edition, published for the
first time anywhere.

Special acknowledgment to Mark Roberts.

The "Hunter's Chant" appeared originally in
Lord of the Flies, by William Golding. Copyright
1954 by William Golding, Copyright © 1962 by
Coward-McCann Publishing Co.

ISBN: 0-523-00378-1

First printing, June 1974

Printed in the United States of America

PINNACLE BOOKS, INC.
275 Madison Avenue
New York, N.Y. 10016

To Manuel, Captain of the real *Christy Sue,* a good neighbor and a good friend. And to ink-stained Ron, who taught Mark Hardin all about counterfeiting.

LD

PROLOGUE

Who is the Penetrator?

That was a question bugging law enforcement officers all across the nation. The Las Vegas police wanted to know; so did the attorney general of Nevada. In Washington, D.C., the Metropolitan Police had a long list of questions to ask that shadowy figure who had blitzed his way into town and ripped open the most bizarre and convoluted plot since the assassination of Lincoln. And the Maryland police had a "hold for questioning" order out to all agencies. The New York Police Department thought the Penetrator was dead. But there is no statute of limitations on murder, and the cases pending file held several counts of first degree homicide open for him, just in case. After all, NYPD couldn't let the public believe it condoned the actions of this unknown avenger. They could allow no one to invade their province of crime fighting. That way lay anarchy.

Since the first appearance of the blue flint arrowheads, half a year ago in Las Vegas, the press had capitalized on the emblem, endowing the Penetrator with a Robin Hood mystique. In an age of domestic political corruption, international unrest, Middle Eastern wars, and growing crime in the streets, a weary people—sadly lacking in heroes—had elevated this unknown nemesis of crime to their pan-

1

theon of the mighty. As surely as the little man secretly cheered the Penetrator's exploits, those who had tasted his vengeance came unhinged at the mention of his name, and lit candles against the day when they might also be handed a Cheyenne arrowhead. It was an award, they all knew, one usually received posthumously.

When the Mafia heroin operation of Don Pietro Scarelli was being blasted apart in Los Angeles, a young Vietnam veteran named Mark Allen Hardin was identified as the perpetrator of the bloody strikes that later became established as the MO of the Penetrator. But when the body count was in, Kelly Patterson of the Los Angeles County Sheriff's Department and Dan Griggs, an investigator for Senator Martyn Corvus, exonerated the former UCLA athlete, refusing to comment or speculate as to the identity of the man responsible. Then, when the Penetrator appeared in Las Vegas, police worked for weeks to discover his name. It was finally provided by the angry manager of a car rental agency. One of their cars had been shot all to hell and they wanted to find the guy responsible. Unfortunately, the man proved not to exist. There was no social security number, the IRS didn't know him, and there was no record of prints or military service—not even a selective service card.

In Washington, the Metropolitan Police were searching for Bart Lowe, who was supposed to have come from Los Angeles. He disappeared from George Washington University Hospital the night before all hell broke loose against a gang of would-be world rulers who used torture, assassination, and mind-controlling drugs. Black Gold turned to iron pyrites in the hands of black militants—bent upon the biggest shakedown the world had ever known—

because of an attack by the Penetrator. It was a campaign so swift, so devastating, and so thorough that even now, a month later, the New York Police had only a handful of arrowheads and a fistful of press clippings.

Yet forces were at work—driven by their greed and lust for power—carrying out a plan so broad in scope and insidious in conception that it would successfully wipe out the meager savings of the aged and the vast fortunes of the superrich alike. A grandiose scheme that would bankrupt the richest nation in the world and place it at the mercy of an aggressive and hate-filled neighbor.

But there was a wild card in their deck—one that would soon prove to be a grim joker—a letter mailed by a dead man, outlining some of the details of the plot and begging for help. It was mailed with blind hope, delivered by benevolent chance, into the hands of . . . the Penetrator.

Chapter 1

VIOLENT ENCOUNTER

Goblins and harlequins thronged the dirty streets of the French Quarter, jostling shoulders with devils and dominoes as they moved in a surging, solid mass, filled with the spirit of Carnival.

Mardi Gras was five nights old, with five more to go; the long holiday weekend was just beginning. School was out and most businesses would be closed from Friday night until Ash Wednesday. Canal Street presented an almost impenetrable human barrier.

On Canal Street, one man seemed to stand out from the mob he was trying to push his way through. He was taller than many of the revelers, and his light tweed jacket, dark slacks, and open-collared sport shirt were a marked contrast to their gay costumes. His longish black hair, full moustache, and dark complexion could have marked him as a local, but his deep black eyes flashed with impatience. He was late for an appointment; he was in a hurry.

Using his shoulders, elbows, and forearms, Mark Hardin twisted a pathway through the Mardi Gras crowds, like the flankerback he used to be. His dark eyes took in street numbers, searching for the address in the letter that had brought him to New Orleans.

He had received the message at the Stronghold three days before, delivered personally by Kelly Patterson. It had come in a separate envelope, addressed to the sheriff's lieutenant, containing a single sheet of paper with a handwritten message. The writer, Pierre Rubidaux, had read in the papers that Lt. Patterson might know something about the person he wished to contact. Would Lt. Patterson see that the enclosed envelope reached its destination? That sealed message was addressed simply:

The Penetrator

Inside the envelope was a twenty-dollar bill and another handwritten letter, covering three sheets of cheap writing paper. It was simple and to the point.

Mr. Penetrator,
This letter is written with hope that you will help me. The twenty-dollar bill is counterfeit, yet it is not. Other fishermen and I have been paid with these bills by Gulfland Fishermen's Co-op. When I noticed that there was something odd about the bills, Marcel Bouchet, the head of our Co-op, demanded I return them. I have some of the bills, fifties and twenties, that I told him I spent. I have a friend who says there is something wrong with them. But it is very technical and I don't understand. He said that you would have to know what to look for to find the bad bills.

For that reason, and because I think I am being watched, I can not go to the police or the FBI. I have heard things that make me believe there is enough of this bad money to destroy

6

our country's economy. Bouchet is going to distribute it!

I fear for my life and my daughter's. You are our only hope. If you get this letter, please come to New Orleans. Be at 723 Canal Street, on the edge of the French Quarter, at seven o'clock, Friday night, February 22. I will bring proof. We pray to God for your good fortune and your help.

From one who admires what you do,

Pierre Rubidaux

The brilliant Professor Haskins, Mark's mentor, had given the bill every counterfeit test known and had pronounced it genuine. The ink, paper, and engraving appeared flawless. If the professor pronounced it genuine, you could bet money that it was. Retired from the faculty of USC, Willard Haskins had indulged his every whim in building his fantastic retreat, the Stronghold, in the Calico Mountains of California's great desert. In the Stronghold was a small, elaborate laboratory that had adequate resources to test the sample bill. Yet there was Pierre Rubidaux's assurance that the nation's economy was threatened. Curiosity got the better of Mark Hardin. Curiosity and the growing suspicion that once again, a little man's problem had grown big and touched the Penetrator. He decided to keep the appointment in New Orleans. . . .

He had found it. Nestled between a jazz parlor that was blaring loud strains of Dixieland onto the street, and a voodoo supply shop on the west side of Canal Street, leaned a narrow, drab building. Deeply worn stone steps led to its walk-up entrance. Wrought-iron grilles covered every darkened window, and the building gave no indication of occupancy. Plowing his way through the tide of merrymakers, Mark climbed the steps and rang an old-fashioned crank door bell.

Silence followed the *burring* of the bell. Mark reached out to turn the wrought-iron handle a second time, but the door was suddenly flung open. Before him stood a slim girl of medium height, with long straight black hair and large doelike brown eyes. Her eyes were open wide with fear, the whites showing and pupils glazed. She took in the massive bulk of the man standing in front of her and her hand went to ther throat, a muffled sob of desperation escaping her lips.

It all seemed to happen at once. The girl tried to slam the door, but Mark caught it in his big paw, holding it open against her struggling efforts. She gave a yelp of frustration and tried to shove her way past him to escape into the crowd. Mark blocked her way as he glimpsed the dark forms of two men behind her in the hallway. One man raised his arm, pointing at them. A foreshortened flame blossomed at the end of his hand, followed by the soft *ka-chug* of silenced shot.

Mark's hand stung from nearness of the bullet's impact in the doorjamb. He grabbed the girl's arm and jerked her through the opening, toward him. Lifting her off her feet, he bounded down the short flight of steps in two strides. Turning left, the same direction he had been going, he pushed out into the mass of people. He lowered the girl to her feet, held her wrist, and tugged her along. She whimpered in frightened protest, but a glance backward showed her two pursuers on the doorstep, and she allowed herself to be pulled in his wake.

Crossing the street diagonally, Mark decisively wended his way onto Dauphine.

Before leaving the Stronghold, Mark, the Professor, and David Red Eagle had discussed the possibility that Rubidaux's appeal for help might be a setup. They speculated that perhaps the survivors of one or another of the criminal organizations smashed by the Penetrator in the past months had devised a scheme to exact vengeance. Many small fry—and no doubt several big ones as well—had escaped retribution when the Penetrator had slashed his way through Don Pietro Scarelli's organization in his vendetta for the murder of Donna Morgan. It was not like *la cosa nostra* to allow so devastating a blow to go unpunished. Two hoods waiting at the meeting place and a silenced pistol supported that supposition. Yet there was the girl. No one could fake the fear that clutched her from the first second she opened the door.

As they proceeded through the crowd, Mark studied her covertly. She was still frightened. She came with him as if he offered the lesser of two evils. As he began to note her features, he found something hauntingly familiar about her. She was slim for her medium height, with a smooth, clear complexion, a heart-shaped face, and big brown eyes. She had a well developed bust, not overly large like the silicone freaks of Vegas or L.A., but firm and proud.

Memory stirred in him, and for an instant, he saw Donna Morgan in her place. The physical resemblance was so great that it nearly wrenched a groan from him. In May it would be a year since Donna had died. Mark still carried her memory. It was for her and for all the other little guys that the Penetrator battled his bloody path through the ranks of evil.

9

Now this strange young girl seemed to have brought Donna back to him. In a world in which, at any moment, he might turn the wrong corner or go through the wrong door, there was little opportunity to admire a well-turned leg or indulge himself in bittersweet memory.

He was reminded that he had nearly stepped through that wrong door tonight. He glanced behind them. The two gunmen from number 723 had located them and were a scant half-block away. Looking ahead, Mark spotted an alley entrance and pulled the girl ahead of him.

"In here," he commanded, speaking for the first time since ringing the doorbell. The girl obeyed without further hesitation, and the alley enclosed them in semidarkness.

"Get behind there and don't make any noise," Mark told the girl, indicating the darker form of a Dempster dumpster garbage bin. As she complied without protest, he turned to wait for the two men.

As the pair rounded a building front, entering the alley, Mark leaned back against a rough wall in deeper darkness. He flexed his wrist, releasing his slim-bladed sleeve knife. Silent and unmoving, Mark waited for the right moment as they approached, the *pistolero* in the lead.

"Darker'n the inside of a turd in here," the man behind complained.

"Just the lights, Jake. You'll get used to it in a second," the gunman told him.

They were drawing abreast of Mark, unable to see him because of their imperfect night vision. He tensed, shifting weight and balance for the attack. It was just about time.

"I don't see anything, do you, Al? Where'd they

go, anyway?" the shorter hood asked his companion. He neared the midpoint of the garbage bin.

"Right here!" Mark exclaimed. The sound of Mark's voice coming from behind them caught the two torpedoes off guard. They turned quickly, but Jake's body blocked his partner's line of fire. Mark moved in swiftly, bringing the wicked point of his stiletto up in a sweeping arc that pierced the little hit man's stomach, just below the diaphragm, driving upward through that dome-shaped muscle into his heart. Jake died with only a startled gasp.

Continuing his momentum, the Penetrator lifted the small man backward, jamming the dead man into the taller gunman. Taking awkward steps backward, Al tried to free his gun for a shot, but it was too late. Death quietly overtook him as Mark released the dead Jake and delivered a paralyzing karate blow to the base of Al's neck with his left hand. He followed through with the heel of his right hand, driving the blow to the base of the killer's nose, his powerful shoulder fully behind it. Cartilage gave way and bone splintered, driving jagged shards upward into the brain. Searing brightness and pain flashed through Al's mind and then an eternity of blackness.

From where she crouched behind the metal bin, the girl thought Mark had used only his fists, pounding their pursuers into unconsciousness. Now Mark blocked her view as he bent to retrieve his knife, wiping it and his hands on Jake's shirt. He stowed the blade and turned toward the girl.

"Are you all right?" she asked in a timid voice.

"Let's get out of here," Mark answered.

Once on the brightly lighted street at the opposite end of the alley, the girl halted Mark, a look of gratitude and appeal on her face.

11

"I ... you saved my life. I don't know how to thank you. My name is Angelique Rubidaux."

"Then you had better come up with some answers. I came to that house to meet a man named Pierre Rubidaux."

Angelique's eyes grew large and her fingers fluttered in nervous agitation. "Then ... then you ... must be ... the ... Penetrator," she said, her voice dropping lower with each word.

Chapter 2

REQUIEM FOR A FISHERMAN

What do you do at a time like this? Mark thought as he struggled to overcome his shock at the girl's response. Do you grin and say something inane like, "That's me all right?" Aloud, he settled for a stalling tactic.

"We can't talk here."

Angelique took his hand, starting off across the street. "This way," she said.

They worked their way farther east, into the French Quarter, carried along by the crowd. When they reached Bourbon Street, they stopped.

"How about over there?" Mark suggested, pointing out the balcony of the Embers restaurant at the corner of Bourbon and St. Peter's. "We can sit up there and watch everything going on in the streets without being seen ourselves."

Soon they were on the balcony. Over the predinner drinks Mark had insisted on as therapy, Angelique Rubidaux noticed the stains on Mark's coat and shirt cuffs.

"That's blood," she said in a strangled voice. "Did they hurt you?"

"No."

Her eyes widened with fearful comprehension. "What . . . What did you do to those men?"

"I took them out," he stated simply. To her doubt-

13

ful look, he explained, "They were trying to kill me, to kill us both, so I wasted them."

"Took out? Wasted? You mean you *killed* them?"

"Of course. Which gets right to the point. You or Pierre Rubidaux have a lot of explaining to do. What kind of setup were you trying to suck me into?"

"My father, Pierre Rubidaux, is dead. Those men, or some others murdered him this morning." Angelique's eyes filled with tears and she fought them down before continuing. "Some Gulfland men said they saw it. That he slipped on fish slime and fell on a marlin spike. But he lived a while after I found him. He said that the Gulfland men had stabbed him. He died before the police arrived and they wouldn't believe me." The tears were running freely now, wetting her cheeks as she told of what happened.

"Why was that?"

"Those others said he had fallen. And . . . well, the police know how much Daddy hated Marcel Bouchet and what had happened to Gulfland. Then when that police lieutenant from New Orleans came down, said he was sent to give the best for a co-op member, he mixed me all up, confused what I was saying. They wanted to believe it was an accident, and that's what they are believing.

"After that, those men—the ones you killed—came after me. I hid from them until it was time. Daddy told me where and when he was to meet you. They must have followed me to the house. I heard some scratching noises at the back door and then the bell rang. They kicked in the door then. I ran. When I opened the door they were right behind me. I was scared and I didn't know what you looked like . . . and you are so big. I thought at first you were one of

14

them. Then, when you helped me escape and stopped them in that alley . . ."

"That answers that. For the time being, anyway. What do you know about the counterfeiting your father mentioned in his letter?"

"He only told me a little about it before he wrote that letter. He said he had proof that Marcel Bouchet took over Gulfland for a front. That Bouchet was mixed up in a counterfeiting ring and was using the co-op for distributing it. He said he had heard that it was so big a thing that it could destroy our whole economy."

"That's essentially all he put in the letter. Where is that proof now?"

"I don't know. He hid it yesterday. He took his boat out alone, and when he came back he said it was in a safe place until he could give it to you. Even when . . . when he was dying, he never told me where."

A harried waiter slapped food down on their table. Mark cut into the two-pound rare porterhouse, eating vigorously, replenishing the energy consumed by his large, powerful body. Angelique only picked at her food, too disturbed by the day's events to think of nourishment. Her eyes kept straying from the lines of people streaming in and out of Preservation Hall to the big man across the table from her.

It was strange, she thought, that such a short time ago he had faced two armed men and killed them both. How could he sit there and calmly eat like that after killing two men? It was frightening being so close to such deadly skill. There was an appearance of smoldering, suppressed violence or anger in the features. Yet his face seemed to have softened in genuine sympathy as she told of her father's murder. And the gentle way he had questioned her afterward. She fought an involuntary shudder and forced a smile as he finished his meal.

"There's no reason to expect that Bouchet, or whoever's responsible for all of this, is going to give up just because a couple of his boys got dumped," Mark told her, signaling the waiter for their check. "With no more to go on than what was in your father's letter and what you've told me, I'm going to have to do a lot of looking around to get inside this operation. Your place won't be safe. Is there anywhere else you could stay for the next few days?"

"Gaston Reevé's," she told him without hesitation. "He was a good friend of my father's. He's captain of the *Christy Sue*. Like Daddy, he's been against Bouchet from the first. He fought Gulfland's takeover of the shrimp fleet, too."

"If he was your father's friend, won't Bouchet expect you to go there?"

She gave it a moment's thought. "Gaston lives in Grand Isle. Gulfland's offices, their plant and docks, everything, is here in New Orleans. Grand Isle's eighty-five miles from here. If I just disappear, won't they think I'd try hiding in a big city instead of where everyone knows me?"

"It's a thought. At least it's worth trying for tonight. Maybe your captain Reevé can tell me more about this counterfeit scheme. How do we get there?"

"Take U.S. Ninety west out of town to State Highway One. You'll turn left onto it and go south through Perry to Grand Isle."

"Got it."

". . . This is my wife Rose, and these are my kids," the bearlike, gruff-voiced fisherman, Gaston Reevé, introduced his family to Mark Hardin. "Anne, Peter,

16

Nancy, Luther, Zina, Carl . . ." He went on to name all thirteen children, ending with Bobby, a bright-eyed boy who had just come in from the yard.

At the introduction, the boy waved his hand in a splay-fingered gesture, grinning. "Hey, Fred," he said, imitating a Negro accent, "how about some Ripple?" It got a laugh from the other children, but left Mark confused.

Gaston apologized. He explained that the boy was imitating Fred Sanford, a character from a popular television show. "Ah, and this is my chief engineer, Jiggs Flobert," he continued, indicating a short, bow-legged man of mixed heritage, who wore a broad grin and high gum rubber waders. He was coming from the kitchen, his stubby, scarred fingers wrapped around four tall white-and-red cans of Jax beer.

"Thought you folks might be dry," he said in his soft, nearly inaudible voice. "Drink up, Fred, there's plenty more."

"Son of a gun!" Gaston shouted through his laugh-ter. "Your generosity with my beer is overwhelming."

Mark had been faced with the problem of what name to use as they drove along the narrow two-lane state road among the soggy bayous of southern Louisiana. Angelique asked him, "When I take you to meet Gaston, what do I call you? I can't just say 'hey you' or Mr. Penetrator, can I?" Her earlier fright was wearing off and a natural good humor was showing. She was disturbingly like Donna.

Mark tried corny humor to break the painful spell. "I'm supposed to be a friend from out of town, right? So, I'm Fred Friendly, friendly friend of the family."

He was rewarded with her bright laugh; it brought more painful memories. Angelique had even white teeth behind full, kissable red lips, and a little

17

catch at the end of her laugh, just like Donna Morgan's. *Damn! I have a job to do*, he reminded himself. *Don't get strung out on this young bird's resemblance to Donna.* They had agreed that Fred Friendly was a bit much, but Fred had stuck, and now he had a label. A friendly, first-name label that made him as acceptable to this garrulous fishing captain as if he had been visiting them every Friday night for years.

Mark accepted a can of beer and the men sat at a battered table in one corner of the living room. Behind them, the younger children battled over what they would watch on TV, while Rose Reevé opened her arms to enfold Angelique and allow her to grieve as a woman should. Mark took a sip of his beer and spoke to the two men. "This is all pretty vague so far. First, I'll tell you what I've learned, and then I want you to tell me everything you know about Gulfland and the counterfeiting." Both men nodded, but remained silent. "Pierre Rubidaux sent me a twenty-dollar bill and a letter saying it was counterfeit," Mark began. "I had it tested in a lab and I presented it to a bank. The bill was declared genuine. Yet Rubidaux said he had proof that it was bad money." Mark went on to describe the events of that early evening and how he had learned of Pierre's death. When he had finished, he appealed to the others, "Now tell me whatever you know that might help me."

Gaston Reevé shrugged expansively, extending his hands at table level, palms up, in a Gallic gesture of negation. He worked his lips in and out several times, then lifted his beer can and drained it with a loud smacking sound. He sighed heavily and began. "*Mon ami*, it is hard to know where to begin. A little over two years ago, Marcel Bouchet became president of Gulfland Co-op. Until that time it had been small, growing a little at a time. He changed all of this. He started a campaign to get all fishermen signed up as members. Then he used co-op money to buy the *Jenté Alouette*, a ten-thousand-ton canning ship, and converted her into a shrimp canner. Not long after that, he started to hire these hard cases. He made loans to men who couldn't get them from a bank, used the toughs to collect from them, and made them join the co-op. If they couldn't make payments, Bouchet took their boats.

"Each new man who joined the co-op took the shares of stock he was supposed to get when he joined and signed them over to Bouchet. You know . . . one of those, how you say, proxy cards? Before long, Bouchet controls maybe seventy percent of Gulfland. Can vote himself president for life if he likes. Anything the co-op does, it's what Bouchet wants or it don't get done."

Gaston paused to open a fresh can of beer and take the first swallow. He continued, "Then those hard guys started leanin' real heavy on all the independents. Like you join Gulfland or something bad happens. Accidents, fires, like your note gets called on you and you lose your boat. Sometimes a guy gets a beating in an alley, or their nets get cut. So, by three, four months ago, anybody fishes the Gulf banks belongs to Gulfland or else. Any kind of fishing you want; langosta, shrimps, pompano, bluefin. From Galveston to Cape Sable, you fishin', you a member of Gulfland."

"Did Pierre Rubidaux join?" Mark inquired, following it with a thank you as Bobby Reevé brought them fresh beers.

"Him? Yes. Me, too. What else you do when you are the only hold-outs? You can't get a shipper to

19

take your catch, you gotta truck it yourself. So you come home some day with a full shrimp tank and find your truck tires slashed, all four of them and the gaw'damn spare to boot. You go to get that taken care of—not thinking about the two hundred bucks that'll set you back—and you come back to find someone's opened the hatch and half a hundred cats are fattenin' up on your shrimp catch. *Sacre nom!* How many times you think that happen and you're belly up? Sure, we join, but we hate that *cochon*, Marcel Bouchet.

"Myself, I do as little through the co-op as I can get away with. Drape my own net, buy floats, lead line, all that from other places. After this . . . Pierre's murder . . . some of us talk today about fighting Bouchet again, getting out, trying to make it on our own."

"Shylocking and illegal proxy manipulations are one thing," Mark said. "Hard to prove it and harder still to get anything done about it. But do you know of anything that would tie Bouchet into this counterfeiting ring? Did you get any of these bills, like Pierre?"

Gaston lit an evil-looking cigar, puffing clouds of smoke into the room. There was droll laughter behind his words. "What is money! With thirteen kids, I have it all spent before I earn it. If I got any, it didn't stay in my hands long enough to see if it even had numbers on it." Then he grew silent, thinking. "For a long time now, six-eight months, Bouchet's toughs have come to some of us and said, 'Take your boat to this place,' and 'Meet a boat here.' Those who do it are given packages to bring into port. They are paid good money for it. It is smuggling, but on a small scale. Pierre said this thing was very big. I don't think this is the way any counterfeit is brought here."

"Just what did Pierre tell you about his proof?"

"Aah! That is the problem. Pierre showed me these bills, asked if I had been paid with any. He said there was something wrong with them, but he didn't say what. He told me the bills were being paid out by Gulfland and that a few days after he got a second batch in payment for his shrimp catch, Marcel Bouchet himself came and asked—demanded really—to buy back the first ones. That's all I know. Except . . ." he leaned forward. "This morning Pierre was very excited about something. This was early, after he come back from fishing. Maybe two hours before he was killed. He said that on his radio he had heard that Bouchet was expecting a shipment of something on the night Mardi Gras ends. I'm sorry, but that's all I can tell you about it. It doesn't leave much time to find out about everything. This shipment is to be in New Orleans by noon Wednesday, a little over four days from now."

Mark asked a few more questions, which elicited no useful information. Then he told Gaston that, considering what had happened earlier that night, Angelique wanted to stay there, that she would feel safer than at home. Gaston looked over his vast brood and nodded. One more among so many would make no difference.

"There is little fishing during Mardi Gras. She will be safe and looked after. I do not go out for six days now and will see to it myself." The wise fisherman's eyes twinkled. "One fine-looking young woman, no? You like her, eh?"

"It's getting to be that way," Mark admitted. "I'm staying at the Lathrop Motel on Gentilly Boulevard, out by the airport, room fifty-eight," he said, stand-

21

ing to leave. "If anything happens—anything at all—or if you remember any more or hear something that will help, call me there. Just ask for the room and I'll get the message. Thanks for the help."

After saying good-bye to Angelique, Mark was stopped at the door by Bobby Reevé's voice, calling from across the room, "Say Hi to Lamont for me, Fred."

"Bobby!" his father thundered.

"Sorry, Pop," the boy replied, only a little subdued.

On the long drive back to New Orleans, Mark thought of how little he really knew of what was happening and how little time he had to find out. It was obvious that he was going to have to get a closer look at Gulfland Fishermen's co-op—from the inside. If he wanted an uninterrupted look, he told himself, there was no better time than tonight. . . .

Chapter 3

SOMETHING FISHY

With a soft click, the lock on the main door of Gulfland Fishermen's Co-op yielded to the Penetrator's lock picks at 2:10.08 A.M.

Getting past the gate guard, clearing the high cyclone fence, and avoiding roving watchmen had proven easier than the silent invader had expected. Dressed in tight-fitting black clothing, he was a darker shadow among the many pools of darkness. Ghosting through the partially open door, the Penetrator closed and relocked it, stopping for several seconds to listen for signs of discovery.

Gulfland's complex was located on what the local people referred to as the East Bank, among several docking and warehouse facilities on the uptown side of the French Quarter in a wide, artificial basin, dredged out of the Mississippi River. It was situated between the Celeste Street Wharf and Orange Street on the main channel of the river. To get there, he had driven down Felicity Street to St. James, parking his rented car on a sidestreet two blocks from the entrance.

Continued silence told the Penetrator his entry was as yet undiscovered. Checking the glowing face of his diver's watch, he moved out, locating a stairwell and climbing two flights to the top floor. Instinct made him avoid the public offices and auditoriums on the first floor as well as the meeting halls on the second. Experience told him that his search would be shorter in the private offices on the third. Likewise, watchmen being much the same everywhere, there would be less chance of discovery on the upper level, since—except for necessary rounds—night patrolmen tended to avoid the extra foot pounding required to visit executive country.

His movements were accompanied only by the soft squish of crepe-soled deck shoes as he made a quick tour down the long hall. His eye selected targets as he passed by. Anton Colbert, Chief of Security, was a definite one, as was Marcel Bouchet's office. He selected the business agent's, Phil DuBois, as the third. Retracing his steps, the Penetrator took out his lock picks and set to work.

He entered the security chief's office first, looking for a duty roster with useful names or for a watch schedule that might tell him how much time he had to complete his search. He located the latter in a locked desk, the drawers of which yielded to the Penetrator with an ease that would have given the manufacturer headaches for a week. The results were not promising. Rounds were made every hour on the quarter hour, starting on the ground floor. He would soon be playing hide and seek with the night watchman. Worse yet, he didn't find a duty roster, so he would be unable to fake familiarity to catch the patrolman off guard if he was discovered. He returned everything to its proper place and secured the desk. Then he set to work with a screwdriver, opening Colbert's telephone and installing a short-range listening device. That accomplished, he left the office, entering Bouchet's next.

In contrast to the Spartan plainness of Colbert's security headquarters—steel desk and file cabinets, hard, unyielding metal chairs—Marcel Bouchet's office had an almost feminine atmosphere. The walls were lined with shelves, filled with china and glass ship models, each one painted in meticulous detail. Behind the free-form blond maple desk, the Penetrator's flashlight picked out a wood and brass cutaway model, under glass, of a ship identified as the *Jenté Alouette*. It was the type of model given by shipbuilders to proud owners. Apparently Bouchet had inherited it along with the second-hand purchase of the canning ship Gaston Reevé had told him about.

A brief shakedown of the office disclosed nothing of value, not even a concealed wall safe. The Penetrator was just starting on the desk when he heard footsteps clicking down the hall. The measured tread drew nearer. It stopped outside Marcel Bouchet's door.

Giving the door a hearty rattle, the watchman moved on past to the clock station. The Penetrator's forewarning had paid off, prompting him to lock the door behind him rather than leave it free for an easy escape. He bent down and quietly prized open the drawer.

Using the huge old-fashioned watch clock slung over his shoulder on a wide leather sash, Benny, the night watchman, punched up the proper information at the third-floor Station One.

It was a routine and plodding job that ideally suited his dull and plodding ways. Satisfied with the boring sameness of his occupation, the private patrolman would never have considered asking for a change of hours or a more challenging occupation. So what if his feet hurt all the time? A guy's feet hurt no matter what job he took—no sit-down jobs

25

for guys like him. He finished his check-in and turned back down the hall.

Benny took another look at the crinkle-sole footprints in the fresh wax job and shuddered. There was something not quite right about those prints being there. He'd been up there maybe a million times and had never felt like he did now. A quick look assured him he was alone and everything appeared normal. Yet there was something, a sense of wrongness that sent jangles along his nerves. He had never asked for excitement in his job nor had he ever imagined it to be adventurous.

Better get Jimmy, check it out together, he decided as he continued along the corridor. After all, ain't every day an ex-con can get a night trick as a watchman. Especially a guy with two burglary counts on him. And I ain't the only one, he thought in gratitude. The place's full of guys been in the joint; my partner, Jimmy, and Duke, Joey, even P.K. . . . But it's sure the fuck weird up here tonight.

"What th' hell, that's stupid," he rejected his thoughts aloud. Too many of those *Executioner* books he'd been reading. Make a guy see things that aren't there. Like those crinkley-looking foot marks in the fresh wax-and-buff the niggers did tonight. Must have been one of them did it. Who else could of got up here? His slow mental ruminations continued as he cleared his time clock at the far end and started down the stairs.

Bouchet's desk was empty, except for a built-in safe. It was a real tin box with a crackerjack lock. The tumblers sounded like falling boulders as the Penetrator used a stethoscope he took from his jacket pocket to work the combination.

Its contents provided no further enlightenment

than had his search so far. There was a checkbook for the Co-op Trust Fund account that had a number of unusual deposits and withdrawals. That might prove interesting to the IRS, but it contributed nothing to *his* mission. A petty cash box containing three hundred dollars was set aside, leaving only a record of alimony and child support payments on the bottom of the safe. Carefully returning everything to its original position, the Penetrator closed the safe. Then he installed a bug and left Bouchet's office, locking it behind him.

Just as he was forcing the door to Phil DuBois' office, the Penetrator stiffened, reacting to a vague sound. Then he turned, just as two men hit him from behind. It was the spooked night watchman, Benny, and his partner, Jimmy. They had come from the stairwell, one taking him high, the other low, like expert tacklers. The three of them hit the floor in a mass of arms and legs. There was no doubt in the Penetrator's mind that he was but a few brief seconds away from capture, and capture under these circumstances would prove fatal.

Doubling his right fist with the middle finger extended in a pyramid reinforced by the tip of his thumb, he drove it into the chest of the man sprawled across his upper body. Delivered at the end of a shortened stroke, the blow was not as effective as usual, but it served to break Jimmy's hold. With both hands free now, the Penetrator used the left-hand "sword"—fingers extended and stiffened, the tips driving in under his attacker's rib cage, seeking the inner softness that lay beneath the skin. Coming likewise from restricted movement, it failed to achieve its full potential. Bruising flesh and tearing muscle, the driving sword forced the air from

Jimmy's lungs, and he threw himself free of Mark's body.

Mark followed through with his right hand, sending a backhand hammer blow to Jimmy's groin. The man clutched himself and gave a high-pitched scream, rolling into a foetal ball. He was out of the fight for good. The other guard, Benny, held on doggedly to Mark's lower torso and legs. A sharp, unfamiliar pain signal flashed up from Mark's thigh. His mind nearly rejected the message. Benny was biting his leg! Worrying it like a puppy with a bone.

The Penetrator slammed an edge hammer blow to the top of the watchman's head. Benny released his tooth hold and gave a strangled grunt. Mark raised his left knee, chopping it under the exposed chin, breaking the biter's grasp. The Penetrator rolled free, coming to his feet.

Recovering nearly as quickly, Benny stood facing Mark, still full of fight. He drew from his police harness a short, wicked-looking billy—illegal everywhere in the country, even for police work. He held it professionally, leather thong slipped over his thumb and wrapped around the back of his hand, holding the club about a third of the way up the shaft. He kept it low, ready to bring it up in a vicious arc to any part of the body of the figure before him that presented a target.

"You nutted Jimmy, ya bastid," he growled as he saw his partner writhing on the floor, holding his aching crotch. "Now yer gonna get it."

Mark had no doubt that the billy club was lead weighted, and he sought a means of avoiding its lethal menace. The fallen man was completely forgotten as Mark manuevered to get an advantageous position. He felt a pressure against the back of his

28

legs an instant before he began to fall over the downed guard. He glanced behind him.

As soon as the Penetrator's eyes wavered, Benny struck, thrusting with the billy toward the outer edge of Mark's thigh. The tip burrowed between the layers of muscle, stretching the skin ahead of it, barely missing the bone. Tissue ruptured and nerve trunks ceased to transmit their messages. The pain was astounding, numbing the limb to uselessness below the point of impact. Signals going the opposite direction—to the brain—were of blinding agony. The Penetrator dropped to his knees, quickly recovering on the right, planting his foot firmly on the tile floor, knee cocked and arms in the "horse" defence. His mind battled the pain, fighting shock and sending confused messages to the rest of his body. Benny rapidly followed up his advantage.

He moved in for an overhand attack, intent on bloodying his opponent's head, battering him into unconsciousness with the lead-loaded club. Mark brushed the attack aside with his left forearm, bringing both hands to the patrolman's jacket front as he went off balance.

Jerking the club-wielder forward, the Penetrator fell backward with him, thrusting his good right foot into the man's stomach. Pivoting through the air over Mark's head, Benny landed on the tile-covered cement floor like a sack of wet manure. Air burst from his mouth and he lay as if unconscious. Mark struggled to his feet, determined to finish it. Swaying unsteadily, his left leg a senseless log, he tried to walk to where Benny lay. But his leg would not obey his commands. It gave way under his weight like soggy newspaper. He felt himself falling and fought to recover. Then Jimmy, the first guard he'd downed, grasped Mark's good ankle, jerking it out from under him, completing the job.

Mark fell across Jimmy's body, two feet from Benny. Panting, gasping, the two prone men faced each other. Through thick, rubbery lips, pulled wide in a grimace of fight lust, the watchman spoke.

"You're gonna get yours, sonofabitch. You're gonna get yours good." Slowly he began to climb to his feet.

"Save it for the movies, punk," Mark hurled back. The numbness was leaving, sluggishly, a burning pain replacing it and, along with that, spasmodic control of the injured limb. Using the fantastic strength-giving qualities and restorative powers of the *Sho-tu-ça* regimen, he struggled to recover his abilities.

It had been a long time ago—January of 1973, soon after Mark Hardin's discharge from the army—that David Red Eagle had first appeared at the Stronghold. He insisted that Mark was, like himself, a Cheyenne, and undertook to heal the physical and mental injuries that had left the young Vietnam vet in a nearly helpless state. *Sho-tu-ça* was the ancient spirit medicine of the Cheyenne Dog Soldiers. A regimen of mental and physical conditioning that, those ancient warriors believed, rendered them invulnerable to the bullets and arrows of their enemies. It had much the effect of *ki* to practitioners of the martial arts. And it had the very real advantages of producing superb physical tone and mental alertness.

The Penetrator focused on those nearly supernatural powers now, forcing life back into his injured member. First the thigh . . . then the knee . . . calf . . . ankle . . . foot and toes. Performing a push-up, Mark came to his knees, then stood, his left leg now taking its burden with dimmed protest.

His adversary was already up, readying his weapon for another attack. The hell with it, Mark thought, it's a good day to die! So closely attuned was his mind to the culture of his Indian ancestry through the medicine of *Sho-tu-ça*, that Mark was conditioned into the fighting attitudes of the Cheyenne Dog Soldier society. Unbidden, the words came from his lips, gaining in volume with each syllable, harsh and barbaric, momentarily paralyzing his surprised opponent with primitive fear. "*Hê, hê, hê, hê-yah! Hokka-hē!*"

Then he turned and ran.

It was an action totally unaccounted for in the street-brawler tactics of the burly ex-burglar. Caught unprepared, his timing ruined, Benny had no choice but to lumber after his fleeing quarry. Their sprint brought them to the far end of the hall, where a wide window overlooked the waters of the Mississippi. Too late, the patrolman realized that his headlong dash had carried him into a trap! There before him, his intended victim had suddenly turned, no longer fleeing, but *attacking*! With a blurred movement of arms, body, and legs, Benny the ex-burglar felt himself grasped at collar and belt. Then he was flying through the air, catapulted off the hip of his enemy. He made contact with the window at shoulder and hip. The inertia of his body carried the glass away, preceding him as he plummeted three stories down to the chill waters below, his lips stretched wide in a soundless scream. Impact with the surface knocked him unconscious and his body surged downward, nearly to the silt-covered river bottom.

Behind the dying guard, the Penetrator staggered to the window sill, carefully avoiding the jagged glass. Night yard lights illuminated the river at this point in the Gulfland complex and Mark was able to see the roiling, mud-stained patch where the watchman had gone down. Leaning against the sash,

31

Mark let his breath escape in strangled sobs as agony ran through his body. Several minutes passed before the corpse came to the surface. Bobbing face down in the oily black water, it slowly drifted away from shore. The Penetrator watched it out of sight before turning to retrace his path down the corridor.

When Mark reached the half-open door to Phil DuBois' office, he saw that the first watchman was recovering from the emasculating blow to his groin. Jimmy was on his hands and knees, his service revolver in one hand. As the Penetrator came into view, he raised the pistol, squeezing the trigger. The hammer slowly drew back. . . .

But it never completed its arc, falling back harmlessly onto the cylinder metal between cartridges. The ex-con-turned-watchman received a front toe kick under the chin that snapped his head back, carrying his shoulders over. He fell heavily, arms flung wide, pistol clattering down the hall into junk metal and his head smacking the unyielding floor. Mark made a quick check of the man's pulse, determining that he was alive, but just barely, then he hurried into the office. Time was running against him now at high speed.

He was not positive of what he would find. However, Mark was convinced that somehow Marcel Bouchet, and through him, Gulfland Fishermen's Co-op, was involved in a very big paper-hanging scheme. He hoped for anything that might give him a lead. Limping slightly because of his battered left thigh, he went through the office with swift efficiency.

He found nothing directly incriminating, but in the upper right-hand drawer of DuBois' desk he did uncover a report on the ecological side effects of massive sea farming, put out by some group called the Green Earth People. Attached to it was a carbon

32

copy of a letter, signed by DuBois, addressed to Carlo Santini—a name that meant nothing to Mark then—calling attention to past difficulties with the Green Earth demonstrators and asking assistance to insure extra tight security on the day the "shipment" arrived. The date of the shipment was given as the twenty-seventh, the same date as a planned demonstration, and the letter urged that plenty of men be on hand, "to keep them ecology freaks off our ass."

Taking a small camera from his pocket—he was amazed to find it undamaged after the fight—he took two photos of the letter and returned it to the desk. Locking the office door behind him, he left the building by a rear fire exit. Any minute now, when the watch clocks were not keyed at their stations, alarms would be blaring all through the compound.

At the end of the chain-link fence, where it came down to the water's edge, Mark stopped. He stripped off the "living gloves" he wore, stuffing one inside the other and adding a fist-sized rock. He tied the open end shut over the rock and tossed the bundle far out into the river. From his inside jacket pocket he took another pair and fitted them to his hands.

Developed for the Penetrator's use by Professor Haskins, the gloves were a tissue-thin, semipermeable synthetic that allowed the natural skin oils to come to the surface. Micro-engraving had equipped each glove with neutral palm and fingerprints. Skin oils assured that these prints would be left behind, but they could not be traced to anyone, living or dead. The Penetrator used several different pairs during each operation, which made him appear to be an army of men to the police and brought confusion to his enemies. So delicate and sensitive were these living gloves that Mark retained full tactile sensation. Only the most detailed examination would reveal them as other than human skin, for each pair had such refinements as freckles, a mole, or scar tissue, and all had a scattering of coarse black human hairs, comparable to Mark's own.

Satisfied with this disposal method, he rounded the fence below the water line and hurried toward his car. From a block away he heard the first alarm bells. He would have to come back and install the receiving units and tape recorders at a better time.

Back at his car, Mark Hardin had just started the engine and was driving sedately down the block when three light-blue cars of the Harbor Police rushed past in the opposite direction toward Gulf-land, their red dome lights flashing and sirens screeching. Coming along in their wake at a more dignified pace was a blue and white New Orleans Department of Police radio car, only the blue flasher units blinking on the roof. The crescent and star emblem on the driver's door stood out boldly in gold and black. Accelerating slightly, the Penetrator drove through the oncoming police unnoticed.

Mark pulled into his parking space on the back side of the huge motel complex and cut motor and lights.

Fatigue and pain blurred his vision, turning his body into a bag of wet sand. The temptation was great to lay his head down and sleep where he sat. It had been a busy night, producing far too little result for his efforts. He resisted the impulse to surrender to sleep, sitting a few moments more, before opening his door.

From twenty feet away, in a palmetto clump, a shotgun boomed, double-0 pellets whirring through the air.

Chapter 4

SPOILED GOODS

The shot was high, hurried by a nervous, inexperienced man behind the gun.

Pellets slashed into the metal of Mark's car, splattering against the thick, unyielding double metal fold of the door post. Splinters of lead flew from the impact point, cutting his face, as the Penetrator dived for the ground, right hand darting to the shoulder rig under his open jacket.

Mark snapped two shots to the left of where he had seen the muzzle bloom. He heard a slightly hysterical laugh and received a second off-target blast from the scattergun as he realized his error. The shotgunner was left-handed! Mark readjusted his point of aim, this time being rewarded with a meaty smack as each one hit flesh. That was one out of the way.

He changed position, expecting a back-up man. Loose gravel, crunching against asphalt, gave him warning of at least two more men moving in on him from the opposite direction. Looking under his car, he saw the pair trotting rapidly toward its rear. He extended his Colt Commander and fired one shot, all he knew he had time for. Tricky lighting put his aim off and the 200-grain Hensley and Gibbs slug hit a skinny runt of a man in the thigh. The impact jerked the ambusher off his feet, an agonized scream bubbling out of him. His partner jumped to the side, making for the deeper outer darkness. He was still headed for the rear of the Penetrator's car. Mark rolled sideways three times, getting away from the car, nearer the clump of palmetto. He made ready for the other gunman's attack.

It came in speeding fury. He moved out of the darkness into the semilight of softly glowing yard lamps. He extended his arm, pistol pointing to where he expected his victim to be, and rushed forward . . . straight into hell. Mark's three slugs stitched an even line from the gunman's belly button to his throat. The would-be killer fell without firing a shot. Already up on his hands and knees, the Penetrator stood and ran in a crouch back to his car.

Peering under the Mustang, Mark looked for the wounded man. All he saw was a pair of shoe soles disappearing into the darkness. Obviously the wounded gunsel was being dragged off by an accomplice. Mark waited where he was until he heard a car door slam and the motor tick over. Satisfied he was alone, he stood up.

Granted, the ambush had failed, but the Penetrator was faced with two problems. A pair of corpses and a shoot-out to explain. Why explain it at all? he thought. Better not to have any corpses around, and if he wasn't there at all, he couldn't be asked questions. A quick check around revealed no prying eyes to later report his disposal service. Even among strangers in a strange town, a gunfight in the middle of the night no longer produced would-be rescuers. The cowardly "don't get involved" syndrome that was sweeping the nation was a powerful compulsion and for once, the Penetrator was glad of it.

Going to the trunk of the rented Mustang, he opened it and took out a pair of extra-large, industrial-strength garbage bags, which he had been carrying with him for a long time now. He went to the nearest body and bundled it into a bag. Shouldering his burden, he returned to the car, dumping the body in the trunk. With the other bag in his hand, he crossed to the palmetto clump and dragged out the shotgunner.

This corpse was small and skinny, clothes worn and ragged, hair long and dirty. He looked hardly more than a child. Stowing him away was rough. The older of the two dead men appeared to be nineteen or twenty, but this one could not be more than seventeen and looked more like fourteen. In his hurried intelligence briefing before coming to New Orleans, Mark had learned that some among the large population of youth vagrants in the city had turned to strange ways of earning money. Broke, ineligible for welfare or, if on it, lacking enough to buy their needed quantity of drugs, they had turned to cheap contract killings to provide a steady source of coin.

Accepting it intellectually did not prepare anyone for handling it in reality. Mark had never killed anyone this young ... except that twelve-year-old in 'Nam. The child had walked toward a group of off-duty GI's, a big friendly smile on his face—and an armed grenade held behind his back.

Driving away from the motel, Mark was still trying to shake the feeling of revulsion that gripped him at the thought of whoever could have possibly hired these young kids for a hit. If what he had learned so far was correct, it had to be Gulfland. But why go outside to hire hit men? Of course, if they didn't know who he was, they might hire amateurs in case something went wrong and his death caused a big uproar. That way, there would be no way to connect Bouchet with the killing. And Marcel

Bouchet was the only clearly defined enemy on the scene. But how would Bouchet know where to send them? There had to be a leak. Somehow Bouchet or his henchmen knew of his involvement on behalf of Pierre Rubidaux.

Time enough to run that down after the sun came up. Right now he had two bodies to dispose of. Where to dump them? If Bouchet knew the Penetrator had been called into the game, why not send him the corpses? Give him a shaking up. So far, the body count wasn't too impressive. If Angelique was to be believed, Gulfland had lost two in the alley, another confirmed at the Gulfland office building, with one more very possible. Sending him another pair of deads might change the odds, get Bouchet to lose yardage and give the Penetrator an opening he could steamroll through. What he needed now was a delivery system.

He had been driving for some while, Mark realized, and a check of his watch showed a quarter past four. There was still ample darkness and traffic was light due to the gas shortage. He saw little possibility of anyone interrupting his quest. The Penetrator drove the unfamiliar streets for another hour before locating something suitable. Two large crates were sitting by the side door of a restaurant, closed for the night.

He made a U-turn at the next corner and returned, pulling into the parking lot. A closer inspection of the crates indicated that Providence was being kind indeed. They had contained seafood and the shipping label indicated that they had been sent to Dominic's Seafood Grotto by Gulfland. He laid the crates down on the off-street side of the Mustang and opened the trunk. He placed one corpse in an open crate and returned for the other, closing the trunk behind him.

Next, Mark slit open the plastic bags, taking from his pocket two blue flint arrowheads. He shoved one of the flint calling cards into each corpse, using the ready-made .45 caliber holes. Then he closed and secured the lids, lugging the crates back beside the door. From his attaché case on the back seat, he took a broad-tip felt pen, making his final trip to the shipping cases. He smiled in anticipation of the reaction this would create at Bouchet's headquarters later in the day.

Using the felt pen, he marked each label:

SPOILED. RETURN TO GULFLAND.

the number of this particular unit in the motel. Whatever leak there was, it had to come from one of them, and he had been in contact with them at the

Chapter 5

BUGS IN THE WALLS

After a scant four hours' sleep and a cup of the powdered battery acid the motel management laughingly called "courtesy coffee," Mark took a long, hot shower.

He examined his injured leg, making a careful, expert evaluation of the damage. A large greenish-purple blotch had developed on the outside of his left thigh, ringed by red-black areas of lesser damage and gray-green bruised tissue. He was tender to the touch all the way to the knee. It took all the concentration he could muster to continue functioning. He adjusted the shower nozzle lower and increased the flow of hot water.

As the surface of his bronze skin was pelted to a pinkish glow, he concentrated on the problem of the botched ambush. Everything so far made it clear that the real enemy, the only enemy, was Marcel Bouchet. Yet, the Penetrator had only arrived in New Orleans late the previous afternoon and Bouchet should have no idea that an outsider was mixing into his affairs. Unless the Gulfland headman had knowledge of the letter. Even that information would not have yielded up the name he was using on the motel register or the car he was driving. There was, in fact, no way that Bouchet could have learned where he was staying ... *without a leak.*

Only the Reevé family, Jiggs Flobert, and Angelique Rubidaux knew where he was staying and had the number of this particular unit in the motel. Whatever leak there was, it had to come from one of them, and he had an appointment with them at the Reevé home in two hours.

Before leaving for his scheduled meeting, the Penetrator took the elementary precaution of relocating his base of operations.

This time, Mark Hardin moved into the tall tower of the Holiday Inn. Satisfied with this arrangement—it had cost him an extra fifty under the table to get a room during the Mardi Gras influx—he made the long drive to Grand Isle.

When he arrived at the Reevé house, Mark found himself in the midst of confusion. Gaston's thirteen-year-old son, Bobby, was home from the docks, the victim of a severe beating. He had been attacked a short while ago, Angelique told Mark, by the son of one of the biggest co-op backers. A gang of boys had jumped him, creating a considerable racket. Jiggs had left the *Christy Sue* to discover the cause of the noise and had found Bobby on the ground, being stomped by the others. He ran them off with a boat hook.

"I'd'a busted the little bastards' skulls, if they hadn't run so fast," he declared.

Inside the house, Mark found Bobby lying on a couch, his mother bathing his battered face with a washcloth. The kid was a mess. Both eyes were blackened and he had cuts on his forehead and one cheek, his lips puffed and split. Part of one front tooth had been broken off by the same kick that had smashed his lips and it gave him a lopsided grin when he saw Mark.

41

"Hey, Fred, ready for that Ripple?" he quipped with only slightly dampened enthusiasm.

The kid had guts, Mark acknowledged, as anger gnawed inside him. This beating was a useless, senseless thing, like everything else that had occurred since he had come to New Orleans. Mardi Gras. A time for fun and frolic, the tourist bureau advertised. It was rapidly turning into a massacre.

Rose Reevé began to cry quietly and Gaston cursed softly in Cajun French. He broke off as Rose went to the kitchen for more cold water, turning to Mark. "Sons of bitches!" he thundered. "Cowards! Why don't they come after me? No, they have to terrify a young girl and beat up on a small boy."

"I'm not *that* little, Pop," Bobby protested. "I hit Herbie Grant in the stomach so hard he threw up. Gave a couple of black eyes, too, before they knocked me down. And I think I broke Petie LaFarge's arm. He ran away crying," he finished proudly.

"You knew these boys?" Mark asked.

"But of course! He goes to school with some of them," Gaston answered. "This is how they work, those Gulfland guys. Anyone does something they don't want, boom, they get hurt. But how do they know we have Angelique here? How?"

"What was that?"

"I want to know how it is that they learn so fast that Angelique is staying with us?"

"What makes you think they do?"

"Because, when they were stomping me," Bobby entered the conversation, "they told me it was because we gave Angelique Rubidaux a place to stay. Tom Girrard, he was the leader, said his dad wanted Pop to learn a lesson. Not to cross Marcel Bouchet.

42

He told me that if we didn't throw Angelique out, next time someone would get killed."

"Girrard," Gaston informed Mark, "he is one big man in the co-op. Captain of *La Belle de Mer*. That son of his, Thomas, is always in some sort of trouble. But with that big boat and being such pals with Marcel Bouchet, nothing ever comes of it. So," he said, changing the subject, "Bouchet knows. But how does he know?"

This put a different meaning to the ambush. Rather than answer Gaston's question, the Penetrator carefully evaluated the information he had received. Gaston's anger and hurt over his son's beating seemed too genuine to fake. It was unbelievable to imagine him arranging a beating for his own child to cover his betrayal. Accepting the beating and the warning that accompanied it at face value eliminated Angelique as well as a suspect. With thirteen children at home, Rose Reevé's time was too taken up to allow her to indulge in intrigue. That left Jiggs, of course, but his show of ferocity and the rescue of Bobby Reevé before any bones were broken could surely be as genuine as the others' reactions. Even so, Mark needed some other workable theory to still the suspicions that had been growing in his mind since the first shotgun blast last night.

Could it be a neighbor? With as much partisan feeling on the part of children, as evidenced by Bobby's encounter, could some of them have seen or overheard something that they had carried to Bouchet's henchmen? What Mark wanted now was a way to end their conversation without making an explanation. He needed to get to his car so he could check out this new possibility.

"What's done is done," he told them, aware of the triteness of it. At least it gave him a way out. "What we have to decide is what we're going to do now. That reminds me, Gaston, I brought along something I want you to take a look at. Come out to the car, will you?"

Outside, Mark opened the trunk and took out a small black box. "I have an idea I want to check out. I'll go through your house with this to see if I'm right."

As Mark shut the lid, Gaston stopped him with a hand on his arm. "You come well equipped for a friend of the family, *mon ami*. Would I be mistaken in assuming that you are the one Pierre said he was writing to for help? This, ah, Penetrator?"

Good God, Mark wondered, did Rubidaux tell every fisherman in the fleet? When he refrained from reply, Gaston went on.

"If I am right that you are the Penetrator, it would be safe to say that *Fred* is not your real name, no?"

"You could say that."

"*Bon.* You have told me and yet you have not told me. This way, if the police, or anyone else, were to ask if I knew whether the Penetrator was here, I could truthfully say that I did not know. This is clever, *oui*?"

"Be careful you don't clever yourself into a grave, Gaston."

"Seriously, my friend, I am glad you are here— whatever name you wish to call yourself. If anyone can help that poor girl, it is you."

"So we begin with this," Mark said, bringing their exchange to a useful point. "When we go back inside, you and I will carry on a conversation about anything. If I'm right, the last thing we want is a roomful of silence while I run around waving a little black box."

The Penetrator swept the entire Reevé house with his electronic detector, beginning in the living room.

"Hey! A real James Bond black box gadget," Bobby yelled from the couch when he saw Mark begin. The Penetrator frowned at the boy, pressing a finger to his lips and shaking his head to indicate the need for silence. That comment could have easily blown the whole thing, but maybe whoever was monitoring the listening devices—if there were any—would ignore the comments of a kid.

"I'm still worried about what you were saying, Gaston," Mark began their charade. "About Bouchet finding out Angelique was here. Do you think it might have been a neighbor? Something they saw or heard?"

Gaston sighed heavily. "I would not like to think so. I have known my neighbors for a long time, grown up with many of them. But they all belong to the co-op, as I do. It is hard to say what a man can be made to do."

Mark completed one pass of the room. He had received a slight fluctuation of the needle as he passed the telephone. Increasing the calibration one notch, he retraced his steps. Bobby Reevé watched him intently with obsidian eyes that glittered with excitement behind puffed, discolored lids.

This time, as he passed the phone, the needle nearly pegged, diminishing as he moved away. Mark covered his actions with words as he made another circuit of the room.

"Well then, I want you to make a list of those you figure are most likely. Maybe we can get the police to look into their activities, learn something that way." He found another listening device in an exterior wall of the room, apparently driven in from outside when no one was at home. It had to be a

45

very new and sophisticated piece of electronic sur-
veillance equipment—or perhaps a homemade,
amateur job. All of the "spike mike" type bugs that
Mark was acquainted with had to have a direct connection feeding into an amplifier before they could
be tape recorded, let alone listened to.

Mark made signs for Gaston to talk and keep talking. The older man's natural loquaciousness paid off.
He launched into a long-winded monologue of pro-
testation, naming each of his friends and neighbors
and extolling their virtues, honor, and loyalty, while
Mark, having located the proper frequency, quickly
checked out the rest of the rooms. He found another
bug in the kitchen and a final one—much to Rose's
embarrassment—in the parental bedroom. Gaston
was finally running down when his wife and the
Penetrator returned to the living room.

"How about Jiggs here?" the Penetrator asked, indicating Gaston's chief engineer as a means of continuing the illusion of a several-part conversation for
whomever was listening.

"Gawdamn you!" the little man shouted, jumping
to his feet, the inevitable can of Jax in one hand.
"You think I work for someone do that to a kid, I
break your gawdamned head too." Anger was roiling
across Gaston's face also.

"All right! All right. I apologize. I didn't really
think so. I just had to make sure."

"Anybody ever again say I double-cross my
friend," Jiggs continued ominously, "it's like anybody ever again hurt little Bobby. I run marlin spike
through them."

"Like Pierre Rubidaux?" Mark asked.

"Sonofabitch you!" Jiggs started to swing, even as
the Penetrator made ready to block it. Angelique's
shout arrested their motions.

"Stop it, both of you!" Tears ran down her cheeks as she walked between them. "Gaston is my godfather and as close to me as flesh and blood and Jiggs Flobert has been like an uncle to me since I was a baby. I won't hear anyone say anything against either one. I won't! What do you mean, coming here, asking strange questions, snooping around with that—that thing, accusing the very ones who have helped me of trying to do me harm?"

"Angelique," Mark tried to calm her. "I've apologized once. I will again. I let my suspicious imagination run away with me. I'm sorry. Am I forgiven, Jiggs?" He extended his hand.

"Forgotten," Jiggs replied, taking Mark's hand. "Sonofabitch! You are brave man, Fred. Not many men want to take on Jiggs Flobert. I'm a real tiger."

"Me-ow!" Bobby Reevé called from the sofa. He was sitting up now, drinking a coke. Jiggs turned toward him. Laughing, he thumbed his nose at the boy. Bobby replied with a rude noise that elsewhere would be called a Bronx cheer.

"Gaston." Mark nodded his head to indicate he wanted the other man to accompany him.

They came out of the door together and walked to Mark's car. After he put away his detection device, he turned to Gaston. "I'm sure you know what I was doing in there. I found four listening devices. A wire tap on your phone, and a room bug in the living room. There was another one in the kitchen and one in your bedroom."

"Son-of-a-gun! Whoever listens to *that* one, he must have one ver-r-ry dirty mind." He went on to explain, "How else you think I get thirteen kids? One very dirty mind."

Mark took out a pen and paper, writing down the name of his motel and the room number. "I'm not

47

staying where I was. That's the reason for all the questions and checking for bugs. When I got to my motel after leaving here last night, there was an ambush waiting. Since the only place I mentioned where I was staying was here, I knew the leak had to come from your house, somehow."

"The ambush? What happened?"

"Two of them got away. One with a bullet in him."

"And?"

"I found some Gulfland shipping boxes and sent two corpses back to Marcel Bouchet."

"Hey, hey, hey! Son-of-a-gun, I like the way you work! Bouchet will fill his pants over that."

"It isn't some sort of game, Gaston. You have too many hostages to fortune to relax one little bit until this is over. Don't discuss the ambush or my moving inside your house. And don't call me on your phone. If you have to reach me for any reason, go outside. Use a pay phone. Use a different one every time.

"Another thing. Be careful of your conversations. I don't mean quit talking in the house, but be careful of what you say at all times. If they don't get wise that we know about the bugs, we have an advantage. I'm going to work up some dandy little bits of misinformation to give them."

"Pretty good idea."

"I have to leave. I've got another stop to make. I want to get some more background on Gulfland. Again, be careful. Especially of your children. They're so vulnerable."

Two blocks away, unseen by Mark as he left the Reevé home for the long drive back to New Orleans, a nondescript car pulled around a corner and out into traffic, following him.

The driver was Chinese, dressed in a Western suit. His eyes were firmly fixed on Mark's Mustang, following it toward State Highway One. Total concentration on his task prevented conversation with the car's other occupant.

Beside him sat a slightly built, pale-complexioned man. His eyes were set too close to his narrow nose and his buck-toothed, sallow, pockmarked face gave him a rabbity appearance. He sat at the edge of the seat, as if anxious to get somewhere or do something—and all the while, his long, pale, spatulate fingers lovingly fondled a sawed-off shotgun. . . .

Chapter 6

GENTLEMAN FROM THE PRESS

Mark had lunch at the Holiday Inn before preparing for his expedition. A dozen boiled, spiced Gulf crayfish, Creole rice, and a glass of moselle fortified him enough to assume his role.

Upstairs in his room, the Penetrator used a short-bristled, straight-tipped brush and fine-tooth comb to work a white, washable dye into his hair and moustache, giving him a slight touch of gray. Next he sparingly applied small amounts of special makeup creams to his face to complete the illusion of fifteen or so years' greater age. It was a make-do job, but Mark realized that in close quarters a full makeup treatment would never pass the professional scrutiny of police officers. Studying his efforts closely in the mirror and comparing the result with the 8x10 color prints propped up in front of him, he was satisfied it would pass. The older man that looked back at him was one of several stock faces he practiced regularly at the Stronghold. Gathering up the photos and other paraphernalia, he crossed the room to where his attaché case stood open. He replaced the items in his hands in a hidden compartment beneath the false bottom and took out of it a stack of cards.

Willard Haskins' documents collection must have been second only to that of the CIA. How the old man acquired them Mark never asked; he simply made use of them. He quickly located two ID cards that matched his new appearance. The first was a Texas driver's license and the other a press pass from Galveston, Texas. The pass, issued by Sigma Delta Chi, the national journalistic fraternity, was genuine and, even though the likeness was not perfect, the bold red letters PRESS PASS beside the color photo and the thumbprint on the reverse side were about as far as anyone would look. He had become Joe Streeter, newspaper reporter. Now to dress accordingly.

Mark put on a pale yellow dress shirt, wide brown and gold tie, and a rumpled brown suit. Next he put on his shoes, being careful that the thin rubber wedge remained under his left heel. It accentuated his limp, canting him forward and a little off the perpendicular. The overall result was a complete change in outline from front, rear, and in profile. From a distance of six feet, even old friends would have difficulty recognizing him. His makeshift disguise completed, he headed downstairs to pick up his car.

When the Penetrator reached his destination, he slipped his Colt Commander from its belt-clip holster and slid it under the seat. Locking the car, he went up the steps to the headquarters of the Harbor Police, at number 1 Canal Street. It was a dingy, narrow staircase that led to the second floor of the tired old building that also housed the offices of a steamship company, situated right on the waterfront.

All the way across town, a subconscious warning system had been giving him mental signals that he was being followed. Yet, he had been unable to locate a tail. After a while, he dismissed it as jumpiness brought on by the events of the past night. As a result, as he entered the building, he failed to look back.

Up the block from where Mark parked his car, the light gray sedan that had followed him from Grand Isle to the Holiday Inn and then across town pulled to the curb.

"Mr. Sowers, it has taken much time and many thousands of dollars to locate this man who is called the Penetrator," the Oriental driver smugly informed his pockmarked passenger. "Our intelligence network is widespread and very efficient. But you have no need to know the details of that in order to perform your task."

"Yeah," Sowers replied in a whispery voice. "But I would like to know how you found out this joker was gonna be in New Orleans."

Considering that their wait might be a long one, the Chinese relented slightly. "We have a man in a position where he is able to observe mail received by certain individuals whom we believe to be in contact with this Penetrator person. He examined the contents of a letter that gave us reason to believe that the Penetrator would be in New Orleans last night at a certain time and place. The rest was simple; a purely mechanical function."

"Yeah, sweetheart. Now it's my turn to do my bit."

"Not here, you cretin! We will continue to follow him until the right opportunity presents itself."

Inside the building, the Penetrator was subjected to the usual bureaucratic routine, being shifted from desk to desk like a game of musical chairs. He explained his cover story to the desk sergeant, who passed him on to the watch captain, who passed him on to the public information officer, who suggested he could learn more by talking to Lieutenant Santini.

Santini! Computerlike memories clicked over in Mark's mind. He had seen the name Santini the night before at the Gulfland offices. It was on the letter he had found in Phil DuBois' desk. Written in memo form, giving neither an address nor position, it had simply used the name Carlo Santini. Now the letter fitted into its proper place. Naturally, the Harbor Police would have jurisdiction along the waterfront, thus the request for enough men to handle a demonstration. In light of what Gaston Reevé had told Mark, the reference to a shipment on the 27th could only mean that Lieutenant Santini was somehow connected to the counterfeiting plot uncovered by Pierre Rubidaux. Given this unexpected bonus, the Penetrator revised the questions he intended to ask.

"Carlo Santini, Joe, glad to meet you," the slender, dapper Italian cop said as Mark entered the office. Hand extended for a firm clasp, Santini waved toward a chair. "Always happy to cooperate with the press, Joe. Take a seat. What can I do for you?"

"Even though ahm from outta town," the Penetrator began, faking just the slightest hint of Texas accent, "word gets around putty fast. Gulfland Co-op's sorta big down Galveston way, too, and we've been hearin' rumors about some outfit called 'Green Earth People' leanin' on 'em putty heavy over here. Anything gets in the way of fishin', there's a story in it for us. What's it all about?"

"Longhairs and other creeps for the most part," Santini replied. As he talked, he was studying this newspaperman from Galveston. There was enough of a "just not right" look about him to make him for

53

real. But there was something familiar about Joe Streeter, as though he should recognize the reporter's description. That phone call from DuBois early this morning! About some guy who was helping the Rubidaux broad. And that break-in last night at Gulfland maybe having something to do with it. This Streeter was big enough, but what about that limp and his whole body skewed off center like that? No gimp could take on a pair of those hoods Colbert hired and bust one up like that guy did, throw the other one through a window hard enough to kill him when he hit the water. Then there's that gray hair. This guy must be over forty. Can't be the same.

"They yip about finding new food supplies," he was saying aloud, "then scream that you can't take it from the ocean. It'll ruin the ecology they say. They can't have it both ways, but it makes no difference to them. Bunch of spoiled brats, you ask me. They're gonna have their way, no matter, and to hell with the facts."

"Any violence so far? Bomb threats or riots?"

"No. As far as we know, there aren't any militants among them. We have concurrent jurisdiction with the parish police along the waterfront. According to their intelligence unit, the group consists of students from Loyola and some of the younger professors. Also there's a sprinkling of older people and health nuts."

"For all of that, they certainly turned out a well-written propaganda booklet."

"Where'd you see that?" Santini snapped. It seemed impossible that this guy could be the one. But how else would he know about the pamphlet? When they responded to the alarms last night at Gulfland, strange fingerprints were found in three offices, including on and around Phil DuBois' desk.

54

In particular, those unidentified prints had been found in the drawer containing a copy of the Green Earth People's rare—nearly impossible to locate—report on sea farming.

"Oh," the Penetrator dismissed the question, unaware of the scarcity of the product, "a couple of copies have found their way to Galveston. Looks like these ecology types might be plannin' to expand their protest."

Carlo Santini was distracted. The answer to his question was plausible enough, yet for some reason it didn't seem to ring true. A cop's instinct? In light of what had happened, any reference to that booklet was suspect. Yet, how could he fit this graying, crippled reporter into the whole scam? Vocally, he went along, seeking another slip. "That's a possibility. No matter what it is these demonstrators are against at any given time, they sure see to it that they get a lot of newspaper and TV coverage. Now, is there anything else you wanted to know?"

Mark decided to probe deeper. "As a matter of fact, yes. I saw in this morning's paper that a Pierre Rubidaux had been killed in an accident yesterday. The article said he had been a long-time opponent of Gulfland's efforts to organize the fishermen. That makes him newsworthy to me. Do you know anything about it?"

I was right, Santini thought. It's hard to see where he fits into this, but he's connected somehow. "As a matter of fact, I can," he said, forcing his voice under control. "But before we get started, there's a little police business I have to clear up. Will you excuse me?"

"Sure. I've got all day."

"How about a cup of coffee?"

"Sounds fine."

"I'll have the girl bring some in."

Santini was back almost at once. A policewoman had just brought coffee and Mark was taking a sip of the strong, hot brew.

"Well, now. Coffee all right? Pierre Rubidaux. . . . As it happens, I investigated that myself. I don't know how familiar you are with this area, but Grand Isle is a small community, a fishing village really, with a small-town police force. They lack a lot of the professionalism you'll find on a larger, better-trained force. There were some rumors that Rubidaux's death wasn't an accident. He was a pretty controversial figure, you know.

"Well, regardless of his earlier stand against Gulf-land, he was then a member, and Mr. Bouchet insists that the members get the very best in everything. So, as a favor to a friend, Phil DuBois asked me to look into it."

"And?"

"It was an accident all right. One of those quirks of life that's stranger than fiction. He was carrying a marlin spike back to a tool locker. There was some fish slime on the deck near the tank. He slipped and fell.

"There were a couple of witnesses. Two other fishermen. Their stories are spotty, but they give a pretty clear picture of what happened. They both saw him working on his boat. Later, they saw him walking on the forward deck, carrying something. Then they saw him slip and fall.

"When he didn't get up right away, they made their way over to his boat. They heard him groaning before they got on board. When they reached him, they saw that he had a marlin spike run through his chest. Internal bleeding got him, according to the doctor. That's all there is to it, I'm afraid."

56

At least Mark now knew what Angelique had meant when she said the police wanted to believe her father's death was an accident. The Penetrator wondered if "favors for a friend" included shoving in the steel spike as well. "Thanks a lot." He was on his feet, professional smile plastered on his face. "I've kept you from your work too long. Sure wish there was something in that Rubidaux thing. But, you can't have everything." He paused at the door. "Just one more question, Lieutenant. Now, I've been on the harbor beat since I started with the paper, so I'm no expert on accident investigations or on crimes, but it seems to me that a person who was falling would just instinctively throw his arms out to catch himself. Wouldn't he? Did you give that any thought in your investigation, Lieutenant?"

The Penetrator got the reaction he was looking for and was out the door and down the stairs before Carlo Santini had time to recover.

As Mark pulled out into traffic, a regular caravan took up behind him. First came a dark blue four-door sedan with three grim-faced men inside. Behind it was the light gray car carrying the Oriental and his pockmarked contract hit man. Mark was headed for the Celeste Street Wharf that gave access to Gulfland's buildings. He wanted to get a look at it in daylight, plan his next move. Also, he wanted a chance to go over what he had learned at Harbor Police headquarters, fit it into the pattern that was beginning to develop. And it would give him an opportunity to install his receiving equipment. Looking around, he saw he would have ample opportunity to be alone.

Mardi Gras did strange things to the city. Every lodging accommodation in New Orleans and for miles around had been reserved for weeks, months, in advance. People were jammed in nearly one on top of the other. Sheer luck alone had provided a room at Lathrops for Mark. Acquiring the second one in the midst of the ten days of festival had been the result of the crudest form of bribery, hard cash on the line. The bistros, restaurants, and jazz parlors of the French Quarter were crammed to overflowing day and night, as were the party places and posh watering holes throughout the city. But here on the waterfront, with most businesses closed from Friday night until noon Wednesday, it was deserted. There were few cars parked along the streets and no pedestrians.

Mark had just entered an intersection on Annunciation when a huge truck roared out of the cross street, smashing into the passenger side of his Mustang. The impact slammed his head against the side window glass and his body was battered painfully against door handle and window knob. Blood trickled from minute cuts on his left cheek and ran from his nose. For a moment, he blacked out.

His vision returned fuzzily as he noticed a dark sedan stopping close behind. Again he nearly lost consciousness, but not before he identified the truck as a Gulfland refrigerator van. Consciousness blurred in and out as he clutched at it desperately. Then he saw two men—the truck driver and his helper—advancing on him, lug wrenches in hand.

Chapter 7

PUT 'EM ON ICE

There was no time for finesse, the Penetrator realized, as full awareness returned.

Santini must have caught on, he thought. The whole organization had to be pretty tight to react fast enough to set up this trap. He threw his weight against the slightly sprung left door, coming out of the car low, his .45 in his hand.

Mark came up into a crouch, facing the three bruisers from the tail car. Two of them held pistols; the third was armed with a knife. A dozer blade would better describe it. It was somewhere between a Zulu assagai and a Roman short sword in length, with a broad, thick, heavy blade, honed down to a wickedly glinting, razor-sharp edge. A single swing could cut a man in half. The Penetrator concentrated on the gunmen first, dropping each of them with a shot to the chest, as the blade artist closed with him.

He carried the bulky weapon across his chest, like a tennis racket set for a backhand smash. In a blow delivered from that angle, the flat of the blade could crush a man's skull and the edge would put a guillotine to shame. Mark's first bullet splattered against the shiny steel, driving the blade back against its owner's chest. The shock wave transmitted to the slasher's hand was converted into excruciating pain.

He screamed in agony, grabbing his injured hand and dropping his monstrous knife. The Penetrator cut him off in mid-scream with a .45 sizzler that shoved its way upward through the tip of his nose. The blademan's eyes bulged at the impact as the top of his head gave way.

By now, the two men from the truck had joined the one-sided battle. Mark heard a whirring noise just before the lug wrench struck. He gave way, rolling with the force of the blow and escaping serious damage. He came over, face up, lying on his back, as the driver bent over him, readying a second swing.

Two Hensley and Gibbs hornets buzzed into his head, chewing his brain into pulp. Six hundred foot pounds each of power straightened the driver nearly upright, turning him slightly sideways before he toppled over across Mark's legs. His young helper dropped his lug wrench and turned away, gagging and choking. Mark came to his feet, filled with battle lust.

Vomiting wretchedly, the kid was still turned away from the Penetrator, unaware he was on his feet. Suddenly the kid looked up, lurching forward through his own puke into the center of the street. He bent down, reaching for a .38 that lay beside the corpse of one of the ambushers. Mark brought up his Colt Commander and shot the kid twice in the back before he could retrieve the pistol.

Mark expelled the tensions of the fight in a long, gusty sigh. He found that he had been clinching his teeth so tightly that his jaw and neck muscles ached. He looked around to make sure there were no curious spectators. His eye took in the mangled tin of his rental Mustang and the bulk of the Gulfland truck. Satisfied that he was alone, the Penetrator gathered up the bodies and dragged them to the back of the truck. He opened the rear doors with a key from a ring on the driver's belt. He found the inside half-loaded with boxes of frozen shrimp. The Penetrator placed a flint arrowhead in a pocket of each dead man's shirt and loaded them in the back. He secured the doors and stepped back to survey the situation.

Another try and another miss. Gunmen in the house, the ambush at the motel, and now this. So far, Gulfland had brought the battle to him, Mark thought. From now on, he resolved, he would carry the fight to the enemy. He crossed to the four-door crew wagon that had closed the trap. Starting it up, he backed it out of the intersection, parking it at the curb. So far there were no unwanted witnesses so he took time to go to the Mustang and strip the used barrel from his .45, replacing it with a new one. He tossed the old barrel ringingly into a storm sewer. Next came the truck.

It started easily enough, but the Mustang was dragged along several feet before the tires caught on the pavement and the truck's front bumper came free with a rending, metallic shriek. Oddly enough, the Mustang kicked over on the first try and limped unsteadily out of the center of the intersection. What had been done would have to be enough for the time being. Locking his attaché case in the trunk, Mark returned to the truck. Climbing to the cab, he released the brake and drove off down the street.

As the truck turned left, driving out of sight, the gray coupe that had followed the Penetrator since early morning eased around the corner, a block from the scene of slaughter. Pulling into the recently con-tested intersection, it stopped, the two occupants studying the area. The Chinese's thin lips drew back in a humorless smile. "He is going to be a bit more to handle than you anticipated, is that not so?"

"Good God Almighty," the southern gunman swore. "I never saw anyone so fast or so mean in all my life. Why, he's a regular one-man army."

"You no doubt saw or heard something about the *Société Internationale d'Élite*, Mr. Sowers? He is the one who, singlehandedly, killed forty men, destroyed a sixty-four room mansion, and exposed their plans to utter ruin." He spotted the opening of a diagonal alley that bisected one side of the next block and drove to it. Reversing the car in the middle of the street, he backed into the alley until they were adequately concealed while maintaining a clear view of the intersection and cars they had just passed. When they were parked and the motor was turned off, he continued.

"My employer is the sole survivor of that debacle. For that reason," the Chinese driver informed the other man, "Mr. Wo is most anxious that this man be taken alive. He reserves the pleasure of bringing about the Penetrator's demise in a manner of his own invention. Over the past months, Mr. Wo had spent a small fortune acquiring leads to the Penetrator. Now we have him in our grasp. Logic tells us that he will return to this place. We will wait."

Mark wheeled through Gulfland's gates, halting the refrigerator truck beside their office building.

To the surprised guard who came toward him, he said, "Get on the horn and call Mr. Bouchet. Tell him there's something mighty important in the back there that he should see for himself." The guard started to protest, demanding answers, but the Penetrator tossed him the key ring and walked away toward the processing plant building.

62

A stop at the nearest men's room washed away his gray hair and aged features. He removed the rubber heel wedge and walked out a different man. Pausing long enough to drop coins in a machine, he pulled a knob on his selection, then sauntered off munching on an apple. Dodging out of the way of a hurtling forklift, he waved idly at the grinning Negro operator and skirted the edge of the processing plant. He found himself on the dock.

Only a skeleton crew was working during the holidays and the long pier was nearly empty. Tied up to the main dock was the huge bulk of a ship that the Penetrator recognized from the model in Bouchet's office as the *Jenté Alouette*, even before reading the name painted on the bow.

Most of the men and women working around the area were busy taking crates and other items into the fish factory and paid him little attention as he moved among them. His recon run was thorough and careful, exciting no interest in his presence at all as he poked and pried from one end of the concrete pier to the other. He paused at the far end, looking up and down the river.

To his left lay the French Quarter with all its pleasures, its few rare gems of pure jazz cast carelessly among the overabundance of cheap and tawdry imitations. Beyond the Quarter was the Algiers Naval Station on the opposite shore. And fingerlike channels of the Mississippi as it moved through the delta to the Gulf. To his right, west of US-90, was the uptown section of modern New Orleans. Highrise office buildings and convention centers vied with Victorian brownstones and the antebellum grace of the Garden District. The freeway system of I-10 and US-90 divided the city roughly into thirds. Behind him, north of the interstate, lay the suburbs, motel row, and, on the shore of Lake Pontchatrain, the resorts and the airport. He contemplated these natural and artificial wonders and compared them to the evil enigma that waited behind him.

Having satisfied himself that there was no one aboard the ship and none of the workmen curious enough to take note of him boarding her, he made his way to the gangplank. Bounding up in four rapid strides, the Penetrator stepped across the weather rail and onto the main deck of the *Jenté Alouette*. So far no cry of alarm from shore nor sign of life aboard. The main deck offered little other than cargo booms and hatch covers. A hatch combing forward of the deck house gave access to the lower decks. Mark took a series of continuous ladders down to the engineering section. He made a quick survey, then began to search the rest of the ship in a zig-zag pattern, aft to forward on one deck and the reverse path on the next.

Immediately above the huge engines that moved the ship and provided power for all of the equipment aboard was the processing area. It was an immense, vaulted area, rising from C Deck up through the central portions of B and A Decks with galleries to port and starboard on B and A. The after section was given over to freezer rooms, where raw and cooked shrimp, lobster, crab, and fish fillets were stored after processing. Forward of this seagoing deepfreeze was the processing floor. Divided down a central aisle, the assembly-line-type canning section ran along the port side, while the narrower conveyor belt system for freezing occupied the starboard. Giant cookers, steamer vats, blanchers, and packaging equipment filled every available space. In one corner, separate from the rest, were racks and packaging machines for drying shrimp and fish fillets to make into tavern snacks. More than sixty people would be required to operate this equipment, Mark thought, as he moved toward an open hatchway ahead. And the millions it all cost weren't included in the original price of the ship.

On the other side of the forward bulkhead were the screening and sorting rooms, where the catch was cleaned, graded, and made ready for its ultimate destination. Beyond these were the holding tanks where the fresh sea harvest was stored before processing. Mark took a ladder upward. The galleries on B and A Decks were workers' quarters and storage areas for canned and dried products. None of them held interest for the Penetrator, so he climbed on up to the deck house.

There he found the crew's quarters and small private cabins for ship's officers and processing foremen. Here, too, he found the main object of his search—the owner's stateroom. Shiny brass letters on the inside companionway door of solid oak read *Mr. Bouchet*. If no records of the counterfeiting operation were kept in Bouchet's office on shore—and an operation of the size that this one was supposed to be could not be carried off without some written records—Mark reasoned that they must be kept here. He reached for his lock picks.

Just as the Penetrator began to work on the lock, a harsh voice demanded from behind him, "Hey, Buddy! What the fuck you think you're doin'?"

Mark turned to face his challenger.

There were two of them. Tall, broad-shouldered, burly longshoremen types, a matched pair that filled the narrow companionway. Hard, bunched muscles bulged under their T-shirts and each one carried the badge of his office—thick-shanked, long, full-curved longshoremen's hooks. These spike-tipped, circular hooks were handy tools and formidable weapons under any circumstances. Before Mark could begin an answer, they advanced on him, hooks out, ready to rend flesh and rip his life, screaming, from his body.

This was neither the time nor place to blast away with the .45 so temptingly close on his hip. The Penetrator was fully aware of his disadvantages. Shots would be heard from here to the main gate, cutting off any chance of escape. Nor could he rely, in these cramped quarters, on escaping serious injury from one of those hooks if he used karate. He had a fleeting regret that Ava, his CO_2-powered dart pistol, was far away at his motel and his silenced .22 Hi-Standard was not even among the equipment he had brought with him. That left only his knives. His thin-bladed stiletto would never stand up to the heavy hooks, yet it had its uses. Flexing his wrist, Mark released it from its sleeve rig, transferring it to his left hand. He took out his Buck, opening it with a flick of his wrist and reversing it into his hand with a light toss.

"Hey, Hewie," one attacker said, "the guy's a shiv artist."

"Saw it, Cart. This is gonna be fun."

They moved in, separating and starting to circle, trying to trap the Penetrator between them. Mark kept his back to the door of Bouchet's stateroom, the clasp-knife held low at his side, tip pointed at the floor, edge out. He studied them cautiously, seeking the pattern their attack would take. On Mark's right, Hewie made a feint toward his midsection. As Mark moved to counter it, Carter's arm whipped out, the tip of his hook aimed at the top of Mark's head.

Just in time, Mark saw the blow coming and ducked clear. The hook slammed into the door behind him, gouging a deep furrow in the solid oak.

66

He thrust upward with his stiletto, seeking Carter's vulnerable, exposed stomach. But the other man was already spinning away with feline swiftness.

They backed off a little, bobbing and weaving, then came on again in what appeared to be the same tactic, but this time it wasn't a feint. Hewie's thrust came all the way in, going for the Penetrator's belly. Mark went down, under the attack, his right arm swinging in an upward arc, Buck knife slicing through Hewie's T-shirt. The blade slowed in the bunching cloth, giving Hewie time to spin away, but not before the razor-sharp edge left a hairline of red across his gut that slowly began to ooze blood.

Mark did a snap roll to escape Carter's simultaneous attack, which carried him to the opposite side of the companionway and placed him, for the moment, behind his opponents. As they turned to face him, he flipped his stiletto end for end, catching it by the tip and drawing his arm back at the elbow. He released it in a forearm throw from the shoulder. His aim could not have been more perfect. The knife buried itself halfway to the hilt in the notch at the base of Carter's neck. Pain, that changed to eye-glazing shock, crossed over the big longshoreman's face. He dropped his hook and his hands fumbled feebly at the weapon that protruded from his throat. His struggles grew weaker, his hands falling away. Then he spewed out a fountain of dark blood and crumpled to the floor.

No one had moved while the big man died. Now Mark was the first to break into action. Switching his Buck knife to his left hand, he scooped up the dropped hook and charged the other longshoreman.

Hewie gave ground against the attack, but the Penetrator was able to close with him, getting under his extended arm. Using backhand blows, Mark

67

bashed Hewie toward unconsciousness with the curved side of the hook. But not before Hewie shortened his reach, bringing his own hook down on the Penetrator's left shoulder, burying the point into flesh until it nearly scraped the bone of Mark's shoulder blade. Almost as a reflex action, the Penetrator thrust upward with his Buck, shoving it to the hilt in Hewie's side, jerking it outward, ripping open the other man's gut and spilling his life over Mark's own hand. Hewie died without knowing it, battered unconscious by the flailing hook in the Penetrator's right hand.

Mark pushed free of the still-warm corpse and panted. Who they were, why they had come here, and why they had attacked him with such ferocity were questions of no importance now. The only point was how to dispose of them and how long before they were missed? With a quick look around, Mark located an inspection hatch and near it a sixteen-inch spanner in a wall stanchion.

He removed the plate easily and found ample space behind. Giving each dead man an arrowhead, he stuffed them into the bulkhead and replaced the inspection plate. The area was splattered with gore but there was little he could do about it. His puncture wound was hardly bleeding and what pain he felt was a numb discomfort. He returned to the door and entered Bouchet's stateroom.

As a back-up to the equipment already installed in the offices, the Penetrator bugged Bouchet's phone. Then he searched the desk, finding nothing. A quick check of the room revealed a wall safe built into a benchlike bunk on the outer bulkhead. Bouchet's wall safe proved more difficult than the one in DuBois' desk, but Mark had it open in three minutes.

Its contents proved more interesting as well. There was a great amount of correspondence between Bouchet and Ramon de los Santos, Minister-Commisar of the Ministry of the Treasury, Havana, Cuba. Most of it discussed shipments, delivery dates, and "goods," but in so cryptic a manner as to be useless as evidence. The most recent letter from de los Santos, however, proved a far different matter. It stated that the next shipment would "be on station" between the hours of 2300, 26 February, and 0130, 27 February. It was the opening paragraph that Mark found most interesting.

My dear comrade Bouchet, the letter began. *It is my pleasure to inform you that the flaw in the printing process has been located and corrected. All future shipments will be perfect, without error, and entirely undetectable.*

Mark also found stacks of crisp new twenty- and fifty-dollar bills in the safe, each in bank wrappers. Scrawled on each wrapper was the word "bad." He took one bill of each denomination and slipped them into his pocket, along with the letter. Then he crossed to the desk and wrote a note, left-handed.

Leaving the note behind—weighted down with a blue flint arrowhead—in the relocked safe, he left the ship. He had only one difficulty to surmount—getting out of Gulfland alive.

Chapter 8

WHOLESALE LOTS

Marcel Bouchet appeared nearly as effeminate as the decor in his office.

His white deck shoes, blue twill slacks, white turtleneck knit shirt, and blue yachting blazer complete with gaudy crest contrasted with the conservative business suits worn by the two men who accompanied him from the office building. He was of medium height, slight of build, and walked with a light, graceful movement. His icy blue eyes glittered with anger above thin lips that were pursed with disapproval.

"What the hell's this all about?" he peevishly demanded of the guard who had had the misfortune of interrupting his boss's morning routine. "What's so damn important about a load of shrimp that I have to see it personally?"

"I don't know, sir," the guard said softly. "The driver gave me the keys and said I should call you right away. Then he headed for the packing plant."

"Let's get on with it, then," Bouchet commanded impatiently. The guard produced a ring of keys and they all started to the rear of the truck. Out of earshot of their uniformed minion, Bouchet asked Anton Colbert, "Isn't this the truck we sent after that guy Fred, who's helping the Rubidaux girl?"

"I think it is. What's that got to do with it?"

"Maybe they brought him back on ice," Bouchet replied, with a hint of a giggle in his high tenor voice.

Unlocking the double rear doors, the guard opened them and stared inside. Then he turned away, heaving up the remains of his lunch. He was being stared back at by the dead eyes of a corpse.

Sprawled in the back, stiffened by the intense cold of the freezer compartment, were the five men sent out to "deal" with the Penetrator. Anton Colbert clambered inside, carefully examining each body. He came out of the truck holding five blue flint arrowheads. "No doubt in my mind, 'that guy Fred' you're talking about is the Penetrator.

"First half that group of kids you insisted on hiring gets shipped back to us in fish boxes, now these five buy it and every one of them has an arrowhead on him. It's the Penetrator all right."

"So who the hell's this Penetrator?" Peter Keoh asked, running long fingers through his wiry reddish hair.

"P.K., don't you ever read a newspaper?" Colbert asked his chief enforcer. "This jerk has been going around the country raising all kinds of hell. Shot up a bunch of niggers in New York, blew up a gang of international elitists—you wouldn't know what that term means, P.K.—in D.C. He even took on the Mafia in L.A. and stomped shit outta them. Now we have him on our back." His pencil-line moustache wriggled with agitation against his dark features as he described the Penetrator's exploits to his number one gunman.

As he listened to his second in command's explanation, Marcel Bouchet's irritation changed to a fit of rage. "Who is this Penetrator *bâtard*?" he exploded. "What does he mean trying to interfere with my plans? How does this sonofabitch get away with what he's doing to us?

"You're hired to take care of things like this," he turned accusingly on the red-faced Keoh. "Go out and earn your pay for once! Stop this bastard, do you hear me, P.K.? Get this Penetrator son of a bitch!" While the others stood open-mouthed, he stomped away toward his office.

Recovering from Bouchet's outburst, the others began to devise a plan. The guard described to them the graying man with a limp who had driven the truck into the complex and then walked off toward the processing plant and docks beyond. Peter Keoh summoned more men, briefed them, and sent them on a search.

They learned nothing from the packing plant, which was a spread-out version of the facilities aboard the *Jenté Alouette*. None of the workers had seen anyone matching the description of the man sought by the security men. Nothing out of the ordinary, in fact, was reported. One workman did tell P.K. that two longshoremen, assigned to the dock, had gone aboard the ship a little while before and not returned. But, he said philosophically, that wasn't unusual. Probably stealing time for a nap like lazy longshoremen always did.

They went aboard the *Jenté Alouette*, leaving a man at the gangplank. Spreading out, the security guards searched the whole ship. It was P.K. who found the gory remnants of the Penetrator's battle.

It was like a slaughterhouse. Blood splattered on bulkheads and overhead, big pools of it congealing on the deck. More time was wasted checking every room in the deck house, but they never located the missing longshoremen. P.K. gathered his men.

"Look," he told them. "He can't have gotten too far. He has to be around somewhere. We gotta spread out, search every building. We'll find that punk yet."

But he was wrong. Their search was fruitless. P.K. had the ten security types stand by and went to question the gate guards.

Yes, they had received the description. No, no one matching the description had left before or after that. Only one person had left at all. A big, healthy guy, a lot of bounce in his step. Went out through the visitors' gate. He'd left just a couple of minutes before. On foot. He'd walked down the block and turned off, walking away from Celeste Street.

It was him! P.K. was sure this big healthy fellow was the Penetrator. He summoned his squad of searchers, adding reinforcements, and they left the complex, forming a grid and checking every street as they radiated outward from Gulfland's plant.

After leaving the *Jenté Alouette*, the Penetrator entered the packing plant. From a second-story window he watched the discovery of the bodies and Bouchet's tantrum. He left his observation point as the search was being organized. Walking past two of the men seeking him, he entered the office building. The Penetrator was outside Bouchet's office just after the Gulfland boss returned. Through the partially open door, he was able to hear one side of a phone conversation.

"Santini? It was him all right . . . No, we didn't get him! Your little tip cost me five good men . . . Hell yes, he burned them. Colbert says it's some bastard they call the Penetrator . . . That's what I said. It was just like with the first two. They all had one of those arrowheads . . . What? . . . No one man

73

can be *that* good! ... If that's true, I want some more protection up here, you understand? ... What do you mean you want out? ... I don't care if this Penetrator's the second coming of Christ, you're in this as much as the rest of us and you're going to see it through. Find some guns and get them over here ... I don't give a damn if you have to go to the fucking Mafia, I want protection!" He slammed down the receiver.

Mark turned away and headed down the hall. The door to Phil DuBois' office was open and it provided too much of an opportunity to overlook. The Penetrator entered, closing the door behind him. He crossed to the desk and took from one pocket a screwdriver and a small listening device, like the ones he had installed in Bouchet's telephone on the ship and the other offices. It was a two-way gadget, functioning as a room bug as well as a wire tap. Its small but powerful transmitter had a range of over half a mile. He slipped the bug into the phone's base and reassembled the instrument. Now every important office was tapped. The Penetrator left Gulfland by the visitor's gate just as the searchers came off the *Jenté Alouette*.

Less than two minutes had passed since the Penetrator had turned off Celeste Street and P.K. had sent his men fanning out to run him down.

Mark made three more blocks before the first pair of hunters spotted him. One of the men stayed with the Penetrator while the other went for help. Soon there were six men converging on him with more on the way.

So much for carrying the fight to the enemy, the Penetrator thought as he became aware of the loose net of men closing in on him. One man was easy to deal with, but now he needed a change in tactics. As he passed an alley, he ducked into it, sprinting along for two blocks, toward the intersection of Market and Annunciation, where he had first been jumped.

Surprisingly, his own car was still there. Predictably, there was a summons on the window. No notice had been taken of the smashed inside or the welter of blood and glass on the pavement. Merely a ticket for parking too far from the curb. Hurrying to the rear, he opened the Mustang's trunk and withdrew a new, experimental, 12-gauge fully automatic shotgun. Built on the M-180 frame for law-enforcement use, it could crank out 450 rounds per minute, with no more recoil than a Thompson and greater range than the average shotgun. It was one of two prototype models, recently acquired by the Little Jap—Sal Mitzuzaki—which had been added to the Penetrator's arsenal at the Stronghold.

Mark stepped behind the ruined Mustang, using it as a barricade as five men who had followed him through the alley rushed out into the street. They were joined by ten more gunmen, five at each corner, as the Penetrator chambered a round. Mark was a little uneasy. Other than a few rounds on the range, he had not had a chance to check out the formidable weapon he held in his hands. This would be its first test under field conditions and it was not the time for a malfunction. He swung the muzzle into line with the nearest five as all of the Gulfland security men charged him.

A musical roar, gaining in pitch like the humming sound of a 20mm Ontos gatling gun system, drowned out their death agonies as twenty-seven pellets of No. 4 buckshot slashed into the men with each shot fired. Changing the nearly empty magazine for another fifty rounds, Mark brought his fire to bear on the next nearest group.

They went over like tenpins at the mercy of a 300 bowler. One man hit the ground, skidding from the momentum of his forward rush, only to be stopped cold, his head dissolved into red pulp by another load of shot. The sound of firing had not stopped echoing from the building fronts before the Penetrator had changed magazines again and turned his murderous blitz on the remaining attackers.

Thirty-eight caliber slugs spanged harmlessly into the Mustang, their puny power insufficient to reach through to the Penetrator on the other side. He unleashed his humming death song, cutting down three men with the first burst. Two attackers, both wounded, were left on their feet. One tottered to the side, dripping a trail of blood, before another short burst swatted him off his feet. The other was a black giant, topping six-eight with a barrel-sized chest and bulging thighs. He had taken a load of shot in the chest and was bleeding badly. The giant shook his head and brushed idly at the shot holes as if he had been stung by a bee. Then he advanced toward his target with single-minded intent. A short, concentrated burst from the auto-blaster literally cut him in half.

Loading the fourth and final magazine, the Penetrator stood up to look over his handiwork. The fight was over. If there were any back-up men, they didn't show themselves. Mark gathered up the expended magazines and carried them to the dark Buick sedan used in Gulfland's earlier ambush. He rested the auto-shotgun on the front seat, dragging the keys from his pocket. Then he drove the heavy Buick alongside his Mustang and began to transfer everything from the wreck to his new acquisition.

Up in the next block, from their vantage point in the alley, the Chinese was urging his hired gun to action.

"Now, while his hands are full moving those things. You can take him now."

Sowers wanted nothing to do with it. "You saw what he did with that—that thing. Fifteen men and no more'n six shots they got off. Didn't you see him reload? No way you're gonna get me to take that joker on alone. He could cut us both in half like he did that big nigger and still have rounds to spare. You want me to take this Penetrator cat, it'll have to be another time in another place."

"Your cowardice disgusts me," the Oriental said with a placid face. "But perhaps you are right. Following an encounter like that, he is certain to be on edge, to be vigilant and very cautious. We shall continue to observe. Wait until we obtain the element of surprise."

Finished with his loading, Mark reached into a bag, withdrawing a large handful of flint arrowheads, which he scattered liberally among the fallen gunmen. He wanted to leave no doubt in anyone's mind who it was that was going after Bouchet and his Co-op gangsters.

He climbed into the dark blue Buick and drove calmly away. The car was equipped with a radio, as was the refrigerator truck. No doubt that was how they had vectored in on him.

Mark drove first to Front and Market, where an empty building provided an ideal site. From the trunk he took two large cases containing the reception equipment for his listening devices. He turned the front door lock on the first try and climbed to the roof. His wounded shoulder was starting to hurt

77

now, hot twinges of pain protesting the load he carried and every movement he made. Working quickly, fighting his weakening condition, he set up the rig.

Four voice-actuated tape recorders were in the first case. The Penetrator attached cables from the rear of this case to the back of the other. The second case contained a multichannel FM receiver, battery operated and equipped for simultaneous reception on four channels. He extended the antennae and covered the entire set-up with an old tarp he found lying nearby. Satisfied that it would escape casual notice, he returned to the car.

Several miles from the scene of carnage, he stopped near a mailbox. From his attaché case he took a prestamped envelope and a sheet of note paper. His brief message stated that the Mustang had been involved in an accident and gave its location. He apologized for giving notice in this manner, but he had been called out of town unexpectedly. He hoped that along with the fifty-dollar deposit he had left, the enclosed money would cover the rental fee and any inconvenience.

From his money belt he extracted two one-hundred-dollar bills and sealed them in the envelope along with the note. He addressed the envelope to the rental company from which he had acquired the Mustang and dropped it in the box. Two blocks farther up he stopped at a phone booth.

It was the Penetrator's first encounter with a New Orleans pay phone, and he had to dig into his pocket a second time to come up with the solitary nickel required for a local call. An adenoidal switchboard operator put him through to Marcel Bouchet's office.

"Bouchet? Just listen. I don't want to hear a word

out of you. This is the Penetrator. Your boys screwed up again. I just left fifteen deads in the street five blocks from your place. Don't send any more or they get the same. I'm closing down your counterfeiting operation. You have twenty-four hours to pack up and get out of town."

Marcel Bouchet's patronizing chuckle came clearly over the line. "Fifteen men dead? Counterfeiting? Come now, this is some sort of a childish joke."

"You're missing two longshoremen—a couple more of your goon squad, right? I don't think you'll find them laughing about it. If I were you, I'd look in your safe on the *Jenté Alouette* if you want to find out what they think about it."

"I'm there now. This tasteless joke has gone far enough," his tenor voice tightened with anger. "You don't seriously expect me to believe you stuffed two fullgrown men into that little box."

"Listen, Bouchet," the Penetrator growled back, "If you don't believe I can blow you away any time I feel like it, you'd *better* look in that safe!"

Mark hung up before Marcel Bouchet could answer. He returned to the car and drove toward the airport where his Beechcraft was parked and to the antibiotics that waited in it. The hook wound was hurting badly now, growing worse each minute. Pain clubbed its way through his body with each beat of his heart.

Until now, Marcel Bouchet had not experienced fear in his dealings with the Penetrator. Anger, yes. And frustrated rage at the seeming inability of his underlings to deal with a single man. But not fear. Not yet.

After the Penetrator hung up on him, Bouchet

went to his safe to find out what was behind the caller's mad boast. He was working the combination when his phone rang a second time. It was Carlo Santini. The Harbor Police had discovered the bodies of fifteen Gulfland security men scattered for a block along Market, five blocks from Bouchet's office. Penetrator arrowheads were found all over the place. And the press had found out. They were demanding a story.

It was just as the Penetrator had said.

Bouchet opened his safe then and found another of the blue flint points. Along with it was a note. Printed in block letters, making it impossible to identify the author, it read:

YOUR LONGSHOREMEN ARE CHECKING
THINGS OUT BEHIND INSPECTION
PLATE ELEVEN. YOU'RE NEXT.
                    THE PENETRATOR

Anton Colbert had just that minute brought him word that they had been found, one with a gaping hole in his throat, the other disemboweled.

Now Marcel Bouchet thought about the Penetrator . . . and knew fear.

Chapter 9

KILLER'S PARADE

Puncture wounds and the infection that often comes with them, leading to blood poisoning, behave in strange ways.

Mark Hardin had returned to his motel room and injected himself with antibiotics. His greatest concern came from knowing that the date on the drug package, after which they should not be used, had already passed. Without his realizing it, his mind was already playing tricks on him as a result of an infection spreading outward from his shoulder wound. If his drugs were past the normal date for usage, they must be weak, he incorrectly reasoned. To compensate for a loss in effectiveness, he decided to use triple the proper dosage—without even considering the risk of inducing an allergic reaction. A person may use the same antibiotic for years, then suddenly, inexplicably, develop an allergic reaction to it. An overdose or an out-of-date drug increases the possibility of this happening. The Penetrator was playing with death without even realizing it.

Next he washed and cleaned up the area around the angry red puckered hole where the dead Carter's hook had pierced his back. Breaking open the half-formed scab, he used a cotton swab to clean out the wound channel, his breath whistling between clenched teeth as he struggled not to cry out and fought to prevent losing consciousness from shock. Once more he went through intense pain, this time as he used a swab to pack the wound with antibiotic cream, compounding his earlier error. All of that done, he had to settle for a sloppy job of one-handed bandaging.

Then things began to get fuzzy.

Perhaps the infection that had already begun, Mark reasoned, had turned to blood poisoning. Whatever was causing it, Mark knew he couldn't rely on his mind to tell him the truth. He remembered watching the news. The excited newsman made a big thing out of the killings, calling it the largest mass murder in the history of the state. According to the police, he said, the killings were committed by a man known only as the Penetrator. Certain police officials were of the opinion that a single person could not possibly have killed fifteen individuals with a shotgun in the short span of time attributed to the crime, and the investigation was continuing. Then the newscaster launched into a review of previous escapades believed to be the work of the Penetrator.

Mark's head spun and he knew he could not leave his room. He ordered dinner from room service. Things were really out of hand by the time it arrived. He ate only a few bites and pushed the rest aside. Wild impressions assailed him and, in a lucid moment, he realized that a drug reaction had set in. He squinted, trying to focus on the color TV that was still on, tuned to coverage of Saturday night's *Krewe of Endymion* parade. Images and impressions became mixed. The faces of the spectators, garish floats, the stork walk of the transvestites parading in drag, all swam around him.

He saw a well-known TV personality, who was

Queen of Endymion. Swimming in and out of focus, her face got confused with Donna Morgan's. No, it was Angelique Rubidaux. How did Donna get here? A phone call. That's right, he'd called her. Passion fumed through bright fever. *A celestial choir hung, invisibly, near the ceiling, singing beautiful, but indistinguishable words.* Mark hungered to hold Donna's warm, eager body near him. No, that wasn't right, Donna was dead. It was the TV star who was washing his brow, caring for him, undressing him. But that was Angelique putting him to bed, protesting. Come back, Donna! Go away, Angelique, he mumbled feebly as she pressed him down in the bed, you're just a little girl, I want to lay a big girl, a big girl movie star . . . That's better. *The angelic chorus crescendoed with joy.* Donna was there now, loving him, caring for him as she used to do. Donna, dear Donna, her long black hair brushing electrically along his naked flesh as she changed his crude bandages. "I love you, Donna. I need you. Why did you leave me, Donna?" *The celestial singers crashed to silence!* Ridiculous! Donna's dead . . . Dead! Burned and dead and buried. That's someone else sitting beside the bed, with her tears burning his flesh as she wiped the fever sweat from his brow. . . .

And the fever breaking, pain easing. Driving white hunger growing in their place, growing and blooming hotly into lust and the crying need to make love. And Donna was there as before to join him. Reaching out for her, calling her name as she tumbled into the big bed. Her clothes pulled from her, flung all ways in their mutual need. And then he was on her, thrusting deep into her, his powerful body driven by their long parting and his need to live and make life, fusing them as though they were one. And then they were driving together, up the long keening cry to completeness ... And then there was peace ... and Donna ... and sleep ... and Donna ... and more love ... and Donna. ...

No wound had ever affected him that way before, Mark thought as he awakened late Sunday morning.

He recalled the out-of-date drugs and his triple dosage. It had to have been an allergic reaction, for his mind still held fragments of his wild hallucinations, yet there were no residual effects such as blood poisoning would cause. He was glad he had gone through that alone. Then his nostrils twitched at the odor of hot food and fresh coffee. His eyes snapped open and he sat up, suppressing a groan.

"I was afraid to wake you," Angelique Rubidaux said from her chair beside the bed. "You were very sick last night and I thought you should rest."

"Were you here last night?" Mark ran out of words.

"All night. That hole in your shoulder is infected. But there was something else wrong."

"But how did you get here? Why?"

"You called the Reevé's. Asked for me, but you called me Donna and said you were hurt and needed me."

Mark blanched. "Oh, my God!" Then it was real. "We ... I ..."

"We made love," she said matter-of-factly. "You grabbed me, took me the first time. But with that wound, it hurt you more than it did me. It was just after the fever had broken. You didn't know what you were doing, if that's what's worrying you." Mark winced as she continued, "After that it was beautiful. You came back to yourself, no more hallucinations. You made love to me because *you* wanted to. You still called me Donna, sometimes, but I didn't care," she stretched the truth, "it was *me* that was making love." She uncovered a plate loaded with a double order of rare steak, eggs, hominy grits, and homemade biscuits.

"Eat," she said, "you need to gain your strength." She giggled.

"Oh, hell!" His reaction to the drugs, the Mardi Gras parade . . . all of it was too real now. "Pass that coffee, Angelique, I need it bad."

"Yes, darling."

Angelique left after Mark finished the enormous breakfast. She had insisted he clean it all up, as she also insisted he prove he could care for himself before she would consider leaving.

Angelique was not embarrassed by his nakedness as he tried his first hesitant steps around the room. She preceded him, keeping his clothes from him until he could walk unassisted. Her eyes glowed with a woman's pride in her man as she boldly examined the contours of his body. She even withheld comment regarding the numerous scars and marks of previous injuries.

Still a little rocky, Mark settled for a long, hot soak in the tub. Then he dressed and went through the Sunday paper. The Penetrator had made the whole front page of the local section. There were detailed photos of an arrowhead and the scene of yesterday's slaughter. Marcel Bouchet, through Phil DuBois, issued a statement. It was a rambling, wordy blurb with little real meaning, in which he denied any knowledge of why the Penetrator would attack Gulfland Fishermen's Co-op. He hinted darkly of some possible connection between the Penetrator and the "sinister forces arrayed against us." To add credence to this baseless accusation, the paper had run a short article summarizing the past activities of the Green Earth People. The general tenor of the article was slanted toward the line, "could the ecology group have hired this triggerman *par excellence* to carry their demonstrations against a legitimate company beyond the realm of lawful protest?" Mark had seen cruder forms of propaganda turned out by the Viet Cong, but this approached a new depth of biased reporting. He snorted with disgust, laying the newspaper aside. He had things to do and had promised Angelique he would call her later to let her know how he felt.

He drove to the dock area west of the French Quarter and parked in front of the building where he had installed his receiving unit. Climbing three flights to the roof, he retrieved the tapes made so far from the wiretaps installed at Gulfland. He placed fresh tapes on the machines, labeling them to identify location of each listening device. As he drove back to the Holiday Inn, he mentally kicked himself for what had happened the night before.

From a tactics standpoint, it was a bad situation, no matter what the cause. It made no difference if he had all but raped Angelique Rubidaux—albeit with her eager cooperation—as a result of fever and delirium, or, as his memory and her recounting told him, they had made love often and well a long time after his fever had broken and the delirium abated. Their joyful surrender to desire had compromised Angelique and himself and possibly the mission. A continuing emotional involvement between the two of them could easily cause him to lose his objectivity, to make an error in judgment that would screw up the mission and prove instantly fatal.

But, to hell with that! part of him declared. It seemed that he was constantly being committed to a

86

DA operation, living each day in a continuous state of attack. He would have to learn how to handle his mission *and* his women, if he was to have any life of his own.

Mark drove on through the nearly empty streets of New Orleans, past the silent houses and bright-faced hotels, their occupants sleeping in after Saturday night's revels. There was time enough to straighten out unplanned love affairs, later.

"... So, we shall rendezvous with the Cuban ship Tuesday night," Marcel Bouchet's voice came from the tape. The meeting Mark was listening to had been held in Bouchet's cabin aboard the *Jenté Alouette* the night before, and reception was exceedingly clear.

"Why are we taking the *Alouette* out?" Phil DuBois asked. "Won't that attract a lot of attention?"

"Use your head. Sure it'll attract some attention, but there will be enough guys out, even with the Church yakin' about Ash Wednesday. Come daylight, we can take on a load of shrimp. The main reason, though, is that we can load the money faster. Eighty million dollars is a hell of a big bundle. We can have it on board, down to the processing deck and canned before we leave international waters. Even if Customs or the Coast Guard inspect us, which they haven't done in a long time, they're not going to open every can of shrimp soup on the ship to see if we're carrying any contraband."

"You came up with a brilliant idea there, Marcel," Anton Colbert's voice joined the others. "Shipping bad paper around the country in cases of soup. But are you sure it's gonna be perfect this time? That

87

first goof they made was a damn fool stunt. What would have made them do that?"

"We'll never know," Marcel Bouchet answered. "The mistake was made on their end. The ink and paper they are using came from Russia, maybe the prototype bill did too. I caught it right away; so would anyone else. Now, they assure me, even the microscopic flaws are out of this run, so there's nothing to worry about."

"I still can't believe Castro's people are letting us have this first big shipment on consignment, so to speak," DuBois interrupted. "After losing so much of that genuine paper in mistakes, you'd think they'd want to be sure of a profit. Just what do they get out of it?"

"Plenty, the way they see it," Bouchet answered. "We sell this first load to the professional paperhangers for whatever we can get—it's thirty-five percent of face as a matter of fact—then we have that money converted to gold in Mexico, by fishermen we can trust. The Cubans are asking five percent of face in gold, but their big payoff comes later. They figure we can unload enough of this counterfeit to wreck the country's economy. When that happens, they expect it to pave the way for a Red takeover from inside the United States, and perhaps—they think—they'll get all of those runaway technicians they need so bad returned as a reward for thinking up the scheme. Maybe even get a chunk of the country, like Florida. They've always had territorial ambitions. Castro's hardly more than a Hitler with a Spanish accent."

"They told you all of this?" his chief of security demanded.

"Only part of it, Anton. The rest was easy to

figure out because they asked so small a share of the profits."

Equally interesting information came from the second tape, recording what went on in Colbert's office. Mark learned that this morning the security force was doubled for the compound. Only two guards were ordered for the *Jenté Alouette,* however, since the entire crew would be ashore for Mardi Gras until late Tuesday. The Penetrator went into hurried action, though, after hearing Colbert's second recorded conversation. It was between the security head and his chief enforcer, Peter Keoh.

"I want you to get this straight, P.K. And no foulups this time. Mister Bouchet has decided that at all costs you are to get that Rubidaux broad today and eliminate her. Those arrowheads prove a connection between her and the Penetrator. She knows too much. Mr. Bouchet thinks she might even know where the old man hid whatever it is he has on us. She hasn't told anyone yet or the shit'd hit the fan, so now's the time to grab her."

"But she's stayin' at that fink Reevé's dump," P.K. protested. "How we supposed to take her outta there?"

"I don't give a damn if you have to snuff 'em all and drag her out by the hair. Get a crew together—if you can find any of them sober—and get out there now."

"But boss," he objected, "it's two o'clock now and I got some pussy lined up . . ."

"Do as you're told or you won't be around to enjoy any pussy again."

Checking the time, Mark added Ava to his equipment and left his room in a rush. The conversation had occurred an hour and a half ago. He might already be too late. . . .

Pouring it on the former crew wagon, Mark made the eighty-five miles to Grand Isle in sixty-four minutes.

Much to his surprise, no harm had come to anyone at the Reevés'. The reason became clear as Gaston talked with the Penetrator.

"Right after breakfast, the kids all started talking about the parades, how they wanted to go. *Mid-City* is this afternoon and *Bacchus* tonight. Angelique offered to take the young ones in, she and Bobby. We didn't see how that would harm anything, so we let them go. They took my pickup."

Mark knew now why P.K. and his crew had not come to the Reevé home. The listening devices would have provided them with the information of Angelique's whereabouts. They may never have left New Orleans. Had they found her yet? "What time did they leave?"

"Oh, it was before noon. The first parade started at one-thirty. *Bacchus* goes at six-thirty tonight. What's so important about it?"

They were standing beside Mark's car. He nodded toward the house. "Bouchet sent Peter Keoh and a crew of hatchet men after Angelique. With the house bugged, they'll know she's not here and be searching in New Orleans. Their orders were to kill her and anyone else in the way. At least it's not as bad as it could be. Whoever monitors those snoopers doesn't report in often. The most they could have is a couple of hours' head start."

Mark made the return trip to New Orleans faster than his run to Grand Isle. He gave up on close-in parking and took a taxi, which he had to share with five other people. At the corner of Louisiana and St. Charles, where the parade was forming, he purchased a mask and pushed his way into the crowd.

His eye quickly scanned the people around him, seeking a glimpse of Angelique's slim figure and long black hair.

"Hey, P.K., we been at this since three this afternoon. When we gonna take a break and get somepen to eat?"

"When we find the broad," Peter Keoh snapped at his underling. "Keep your mind off your gut, Fats, and keep lookin." Jeez! The rummies and stumblebums he'd had to settle for on this job. It was enough to drive a guy up a wall. Half of 'em couldn't even find their butt without a guide, let alone one good-lookin' broad among streets full of good-lookin' broads. All the best guys were out tyin' one on or gettin' laid for the holiday . . . Hell, that's what he oughtta be doin', instead of traipsin' through mobs of dummies all day. Shoulda called this one off soon as they found out she wasn't in Grand Isle like they thought.

Shit! The parade's startin'. Better hurry this up or everybody'll be leavin' and we'll have to go clear to hell out to Grand Isle to nab her. Why hadn't someone thought of that before? We coulda waited out there and nabbed her when she got back. But Mister Big Bouchet wants her right now, so we chase our tails through all the tourists and maybe not find her at all. Ha! That's a good one. Like that hairy fag used to sing, tiptoe through the tourists.

Look at all them weirdos out there. Decked out in those fancy costumes, musta cost them three-four C's, just so's they can strut through the streets and get blasted at the Maskers Ball.

Gawdamn! Lookin' at all them floats won't find the Rubidaux chick. She sure is one stone fox. Wonder if there'll be time for a little fun before we finish her off?

Ironically enough, the Penetrator found Angelique and the Reevé children standing nearly in front of 723 Canal Street, where his involvement had started two nights before. He worked his way through the spectators, lifting his mask as he took her arm. She jumped at his touch, then recognized him.

"Angelique, we have to get out of here. Bouchet sent his hoods after you. Get the kids and let's go."

There was a shout from across the street and a commotion among the onlookers as P.K. spotted Angelique. He began to work his way toward the curb, waving his hands to call in his men. Mark grabbed up the smallest Reevé, holding her close to his chest, and turned around. Angelique and the other youngsters followed on his heel, Bobby bringing up the rear. Their escape was cut off to left and right by other searchers moving in. The Penetrator looked around him, seeking a way out.

P.K.'s progress was held up temporarily by the parade and the packed crowd. It would buy them a little time, but there seemed no way to avoid their pursuers. The parade? Why not ride out of the reach of Gulfland's goon squad? At least it would give Angelique and the kids a chance to get clear of danger while he handled the hunters.

Reversing direction, he urged the others back toward the street. Angry shouts came from resentful spectators as they forced their way out into Canal Street. Mark lifted the small girl up onto a passing float and, keeping pace, handed up one after another, until all of the Reevé kids were aboard except Bobby. More angry voices called out as P.K. and his hoods pushed their way clear of the spectators. They saw what was happening and lunged after their retreating quarry. Now, as they scrabbled to catch up, anger turned to laughter and applause. The crowd thought it was an act, part of the show. Angelique and Bobby Reevé were the last to clamber onto the float. Mark looked behind, seeing two of the triggermen sprinting dangerously close. He jumped upward, onto the platform.

Fingernails gouged the leather of one shoe, hands grabbing to drag the Penetrator back off the moving vehicle. Throwing his weight onto his chest, holding on with both hands, Mark lashed out with his free foot, catching the speedy gunman on his forehead with the heel. He fell away with a grunt. Mark was quickly aboard and turned around, facing their pursuers. He reached under his coat, drawing Ava and charging the weapon. He was thankful that Professor Haskins had yielded to his insistence that the dart pistol needed modification. Until the added refinement of mechanical linkage to the slide catch, the weapon had been nearly a single-shot piece. A bypass tube did divert enough CO_2 to open the slide, but the slide catch had to be released by the shooter to chamber another round. Now it functioned as an autoloader.

Holding Ava to the side, unseen by the crowd, Mark triggered off one dart after another until the hunting party were helpless, writhing forms lying in the soiled street. They were far away in slumber before the float was a block down the street.

It was a temporary victory at best. Because of the many innocent bystanders, Mark had loaded Ava with darts filled with the pentothal and M-99 mixture. A neural agent that induced muscle spasms held each victim until unconsciousness descended. For the time being, they were safe. Half a block further on, the Penetrator helped everyone down from the gaudy float and they disappeared into the crowd.

Two hours later Mark stood with Gaston Reevé outside the fisherman's home in Grand Isle. He made his point with no opening for argument.

"With those bugs in your house, they'll know Angelique is back here," he told Gaston. "That's how they knew to look in New Orleans today, as you know. There's no telling what they might do to your family. All of you had better move out of here for the time being. Anywhere you're not known will do. Give a false name and stay there."

Gaston bristled, throwing out his chest, eyes filled with anger. "I do not run away from anything. These *cochons* hired by Bouchet do not frighten Gaston Reevé." His breath came out in a heavy sigh. Giving a Gallic shrug, he went on in a softer voice. "But children are another thing. There is a small hotel in Golden Meadow. We will stay there until this is over."

"I've been trying to think of something to do that will give us more time," Mark told him. "There may be a way to cripple Bouchet's operation enough to slow them down. At least long enough to get what I need to expose their whole deal. I'll need some scuba gear. Do you know anyone with a wet suit, tanks, mask, and fins? I need them now, tonight."

"Humm. There is my cousin. He has these things. But, he is not so big as you. The fit . . ."

"I'll settle for any rough fit. I have a little underwater work to do tonight . . ."

94

Chapter 10

JENTÉ ALOUETTE

It was going to be one hell of a big explosion! Gulfland's whole can of worms might well be upset by this night's work.

Enough years had gone by that preparing for this method of attack had taken considerable practice. After three dry runs, the Penetrator was confident that his body had indeed remembered a skill his conscious mind had forgotten. The phone call he had made to the West coast had paid off with the name of an illegal arms dealer who, after some cautious sparring, provided Mark Hardin with a close approximation of the explosives he had ordered. Gathering up a few other items, he had hurried to the banks of the Mississippi.

A mild discomfort persisted even in the water and his freedom of movement was restricted in some directions. As Gaston had said, the borrowed wet suit had been made for a smaller man. He used it more for concealment than to offer protection from the waters of the harbor and he had to endure the discomfort as a necessary evil. Air tanks were a bulky weight on his back and the once-familiar feel of mouthpiece and face mask seemed alien and confining. The faint salty taste and flavor of cold rubber that clung to the breathing apparatus reminded him that it was he who was the alien, entering a strange and hostile environment for the fourth time that night. This river-front harbor, that comprised the port of New Orleans, was fourteen years and a couple of thousand miles removed from the cold waters of the Pacific, where he and Sean Patrick Michael Doolin, Jr. had first taken up the art of scuba.

As a sophomore at San Fernando High School he had eeled his muscular young body through the water with practiced ease. He made the transition from swimming-pool training sessions to the depths off Malibu with none of the usual mishaps common to the tyro. Sean Patrick, eldest son of his policeman foster father, and he had spent nearly every weekend that winter and all of one summer far down in the blue-green waters of the Pacific, living—if only in imagination—the adventures of Jacques Costeau or the danger-charged clearing of invasion beaches with the intrepid men of the UDT. Now it was time to put these experiences and others learned in the army to practical use.

Making a final check of his reserve supply of air, the Penetrator entered the water backward, waddling awkwardly in his fins, dragging a large satchel with him. In order to effect his approach unobserved, he had been forced to select a spot from which he had nearly a half-mile swim before coming alongside the *Jenté Alouette*. At best, this was only a delaying action, buying time until he could force the enemy's hand—unearth enough hard facts to insure that nothing like their scheme could happen again. With only some forty-eight hours remaining, he had been compelled to pursue this risky tactic, hoping that it would prove costly to the enemy.

As he placed the breathing tube in his mouth and lowered the faceplate, the Penetrator took a final look around before slipping below the calm, oil-

slicked surface. Styrofoam blocks provided a slight
negative buoyancy to the heavy satchel, making it
even easier to tow through the water. His mind went
quickly over his preparations for this attack, satisfied
that everything necessary had been provided. Ghosting through underwater darkness, an interrupted
trail of silvery bubbles marking his progress, he was
reminded of the now-famous speech made by
George Patton to his troops. The general didn't want
to get any messages saying that they were holding
their position, his men were told on the eve of their
departure for the war in Europe. They were to be
advancing constantly and not interested in holding
onto anything, except the enemy ... It had worked
well enough in North Africa, Sicily, and all across
Europe. It would, the Penetrator believed, work well
enough for him. Until now, he had not been able to
choose his own terrain. The enemy, so far, had carried the battle to him. From this point on, the Penetrator determined to reverse this situation and push
Bouchet so hard he'd not have time to think or act,
only retreat until all resistance crumbled.

Once alongside the huge canning ship, the Penetrator surfaced long enough to orient himself, then
flowed downward, one hand lightly guiding him
along the curve of the slanting steel hull. When he
reached the keel, he turned aft and drew himself
along toward the rudder, keeping at arm's length
from betraying contact with the ship's skin. Using a
carry strap, he secured the satchel to a rudder stanchion, fastening its snap swivel to a small D-ring on
the canvas cover. Working slowly to conserve energy
and thus emit fewer telltale bubbles, the Penetrator
removed a heavy circular object from inside the
satchel. He glided through the water to the forward
end of the screw, at the point where one great

propeller shaft emerged from its shaft alley. Moving with caution, he attached the limpet mine just below the point at which the propeller shaft protruded from the hull. He then repeated this for the other screw. The half dozen mines in the satchel would be only a beginning. This was the first of three trips he would have to make in order to place sufficient charges to take out the ship. Checking his watch, he set the timers to allow adequate time for positioning the other mines and to make two round-trip journeys to acquire twelve more and install them along half the length of the two-hundred-foot keel. Additional time was allowed, in order that he could accomplish the secondary portion of his mission of destruction. In all, he gave himself two hours and twenty-eight minutes—cutting his time dangerously short.

Swimming faster now toward the bow, the Penetrator attached limpets to opposing sides of the keel some five feet apart, creating a zig-zag pattern that would end just aft of the midships line. At each mine, before turning the large, inset handle that actuated the timer, he consulted his watch and computed the time differential he would have to use. Limited by the number and type of explosive charges he had been able to acquire from the dubious and barely trusting dealer in illegal arms, it was vital they all detonate at as near the same instant as possible. This sudden, jarring effect along the spine of the ship, coupled with secondary detonations from inside, would be the end of the *Jenté Alouette*.

Time seemed to dissolve away to watery nothingness in the near total darkness of the the New Orleans estuary. As he was returning to the ship with the final load of mines, the Penetrator felt an increasing sense of urgency. Nearly two hours had passed. Had he set the timers correctly? Was there enough time for the next step ... or would he still be aboard the Gulfland canner ship, caught in his own pulverizing blast? Literally hoist with his own petard? His mind began to wander, rejecting thoughts of uncertainty and failure ...

We are going to hold him by the nose and kick him in the ass ... we're gonna kick the hell out of him all the time and we're gonna go through him like shit through a goose, General Patton recommended to his men as the proper way to deal with an enemy. So far tonight, the Penetrator had meticulously followed that advice.

Recognizing the darker bulk of the ship looming before him, he quickly ran through the discipline of *Sho-tu-ça*, mastering his runaway thoughts and returning to a solitary concentration on his objective ...

Once the last charge was in place on the exterior of the vessel, he removed his air tanks, fins, and weight belt, securing them to the rudder. The bulky gear would prove a hindrance on board. The Penetrator surfaced and swam to an access ladder—four steel rungs welded below the water-level loading hatch—and climbed out. The hatchway was open, to provide air to the lower decks and eliminate the overpowering stench of shrimp. It was a made-to-order entry port for the Penetrator. The entire ship's crew was ashore for the celebration of Mardi Gras, leaving only two company guards at the gangway. Far from the main gate, deep inside the Gulfland complex, their presence was more a formality than a necessity. With the increased security forces throughout the complex as a result of the Penetrator's attack the previous day, unauthorized persons could never get past the gate, let alone onto the dock, and there was no reason to expect trouble to emerge from the water.

Soundlessly, on the rubber soles of his wet-suit boots, he moved about the ship with little chance of discovery. A few minutes in the dim light of the blue night lamps accustomed his vision to the interior of the ship. Clutching the canvas bag containing fifty pounds of explosives, he headed toward the engineering section.

Two decks down, the Penetrator took a final ladder that gave him access to the shaft alley. Self-consciously checking the time again—he had forty minutes—he began to place charges of C-4 on support beams and lower bearing mounts along the length of the propeller shafts. Switching to the other shaft alley, he continued the procedure. Each quarter-pound block of the plastique was molded into a diamond pack for cutting effect on the steel supports. A small detonator, designed for remote firing by radio signal, was pressed into each charge and its thin wire antenna extended to maximum length to insure reception. He had been assured by the illegal arms dealer from whom he had purchased them—a friend of Sal Mitzuzaki—that the radio detonators would function through up to a half inch of homogenous armor plate. The sides of a structure built of plate or the bulkheads of a ship would provide no barrier at all. The time for testing this guarantee was drawing nearer.

When the last charge was set and fused, the Penetrator climbed out of the shaft alley. He hurried directly to the open hatchway. Taking a feet-first drop into the water, he swam to his scuba gear and buckled on weights and tank, using air from his mouthpiece to clear the face plate. The seconds were ticking away rapidly. Using his wrist compass for guidance, he began swiftly to cover the distance to where the captured Gulfland Buick was hidden. As he swam, he considered the tactical situation which had developed since his arrival in New Orleans two days before:

Marcel Bouchet, head of Gulfland Fishermen's Co-op and owner of the *Jenté Alouette*, was in for another surprise. To the Penetrator's way of thinking, the destruction of Bouchet's ship, however, was a logical result of the owner's actions. Had his lust for power and money not driven him into participating in this counterfeit scheme, he would not be in the process of losing a fifty-two-and-a-half million dollar investment. Or, if Pierre Rubidaux had lived, the proof he had obtained of this fantastic design would have convinced the authorities and steps would have been taken to prevent it. Then it would have been unnecessary for the Penetrator to sink a ten-thousand-ton canning ship. He would, in fact, never have needed to come to New Orleans. But Rubidaux had been murdered and, with his death went the location of the all-important proof. Even then, had Bouchet chosen not to send his henchmen after Rubidaux's beautiful daughter, Angelique, the Penetrator's brand of justice might have been avoided. Bouchet's precipitous action in ordering men to locate the girl and eliminate her, added to everything else, had placed him on the receiving end of an explosive hell, delivered by the Penetrator ...

When he climbed from the water, the Penetrator removed his wet suit and quickly dressed, stowing all traces of his activities in the trunk of the Buick and removing a small black box before closing the lid. He extended a slim antenna and unlocked the safety circuit with a small key. Checking the time once more, he held his thumb over a concave button. As the watch hand moved to the predetermined second, he pressed the button . . .

It was a magnificent explosion! Detonated by the radio signal, the plastique explosive charges ripped through steel and below them the mines placed alongside the keel went off nearly as one. Bright yellow flames, tinged with blue, shot upward through the ship and water churned around its sides. The sound of the explosions reached him, half a mile away, just as geysers of water shot out from under the hull, throwing mud and smoke higher than the cargo booms mounted on deck. If anyone could have survived below decks or in the bilges, they would have seen the heavy concentration of charges, aided by limpet mines placed outside the hull plates, sever and buckle huge support beams and rip out the hull plates themselves, releasing the gigantic propeller shafts, which, weighted by the huge bronze screws, gave way, tearing out the bottom of the ship, keel and all, to a point just beyond the midships line. In less than a minute, the magnificent canning vessel became a hulk, reduced to scrap metal fit only for salvage crews. In five minutes, the bow rose serenely into the air as the ship settled at the stern, snapping huge hawsers and ripping bollards from the dock, until it touched bottom.

Pausing long enough for a backward look at the flames gobbling up the *Jenté Alouette*'s superstructure, the Penetrator drove away, headed for a brief night's sleep.

Chapter 11

SNEAKIN' AND PEEKIN'

"Here's Vic Barry to give you on-the-spot coverage of the maritime disaster at the Gulfland Co-op Wharf ... Vic."

"Thank you, Chet. Fires are still raging through the superstructure of Gulfland's multi-million-dollar canner ship, the *Jenté Alouette*. Fire Chief Dave Margolis says there is no question but that the ship is a total loss. Preliminary reports from the arson squad indicate that the explosions that ripped through the vessel early this morning were caused by set explosives ... a deliberate act of an unknown bomber ..." The camera zoomed in past newscaster Barry, getting in close on firemen aiming a fog nozzle at a sheet of white-hot flame licking at the sagging metal plates of the *Jenté Alouette*'s deck house. "... So far, the only word we received from Gulfland executives is a terse, 'No comment,'" Barry's voice continued off-camera. "Twelve pieces of fire-fighting equipment, including two fire boats, have been involved in containing the blaze since three A.M. We'll keep you up-to-date on events as they occur here at the scene. This is Vic Barry returning you to Chet Cunningham, for more on the local scene on this Monday morning edition of Sunup News."

Mark Hardin reached out and pressed a small button. Chet Cunningham and the Sunup News dwindled to a small white dot and were gone. The Penetrator flipped on his tape recorder to listen to the tapes taken from his hidden receiving unit. The panic-ridden conversations, recorded since he destroyed the *Jenté Alouette*, could have filled ten new pages in the *Dictionary of American Slang*. Most of the profanity was about or directed at the Penetrator, yet one conversation, calmer than the rest, presented information that told him his job was far from over.

From the bug planted in Marcel Bouchet's office, he learned that, with only slight revisions, their plans for the bogus money would go on, despite loss of the canning ship. They would use a hundred-ton boat, *La Belle de Mer*, that belonged to a trustworthy co-op member, Paul Girrard, to bring it in and would can it at night in the processing plant. It was the same Girrard, the Penetrator recalled, whose son had led the gang of punks that beat up Bobby Reevé.

Next Bouchet received a phone call that was somewhat indistinct, nearly fading out completely at some points. This would probably be the last useful information gained. Although voice actuated, the listening devices were extremely small and, with frequent use, rapidly drained the batteries that powered them. That final message, however, was clear enough, as Bouchet learned from Anton Colbert that not only had P.K. failed to capture Angelique Rubidaux, but that he and his crew had to be bailed out of jail. They had been charged with disorderly conduct after police apprehended them, sound asleep, in the middle of Canal Street, during the *Bacchus* parade.

Bouchet's earlier conversation and the decision to continue with the counterfeiting operation was cause for considerable worry. The penetrator realized he could simply kill Bouchet and the other men behind the plot, but, like sinking the *Jenté Alouette*, it would be at best a temporary measure. It was the counterfeit money itself that presented the real problem. Bouchet had already hinted that enough of it was being printed to wreck the economy. Mark had little reason to doubt that statement. No matter how strong the dollar might be, this vast sum of phony money, so perfect that clues known only to a dead man could give them the means of detecting it, would spell instant panic, monetary confusion, and eventual disaster.

With as much effort as had gone into the project so far, it stood to reason that the Cubans would find another means of distribution if Bouchet was removed and exploit the idea fully. The result would be tragic. Somehow, the whole problem had to be resolved in a manner that would leave no doubt about foreign involvement.

Pulling himself from his thoughts, Mark left his room. It was time for another reecee of the area.

It looked like Pearl Harbor in miniature around the Gulfland wharf.

All but three units—two pumpers and a fire boat—had been withdrawn, but evidence of the destruction was everywhere. Every pane of glass in the packing plant was broken and many along the near face of the office building as well. Billows of steam and occasional streamers of gray-black smoke rose beyond the processing plant, from where the ruined ship lay, decks awash, only the pilot house showing above water. From his covert position in a recessed doorway across the street, the Penetrator studied the situation. He noted the increased number of guards and plainclothes security men, keeping track of their patrol patterns and relief schedules. Dogs had been added, too. As he stored this information for future reference, part of Mark's mind was weighing the facts and suppositions he had acquired so far.

There had to be a weak link. Some flaw in their operation that was known to Bouchet, but that he had so far missed. There had been little enough time for thought since Friday night. He had been in the attack or fighting off the enemy since hardly an hour after his arrival in New Orleans. Whatever their weakness, it had to revolve around Angelique. No matter how much provocation the Penetrator offered them, how great the damage he caused, they continued to go after the girl. Bouchet's single-minded insistence that Angelique be killed had to mean that he was convinced she knew something of real danger to him and his partners.

That something had to be the content or whereabouts of the documents her father had assembled linking Bouchet and the Gulfland officials with the Cuban counterfeit scheme. Nothing else would explain Bouchet's attitude. Simple revenge was meaningless in light of their plans. Yet, if she possessed such knowledge, the girl was totally unaware of it. Unless she knew something, the time element alone argued against anything so irrational as vengeance.

What about the evidence itself? What could a fisherman—by his own admission ignorant of technical details—have discovered that missed detection in a laboratory? The twenty-dollar bill Rubidaux had sent to the Penetrator had been okayed by a bank official and given Willard Haskins' seal of approval. Maybe that's where his answer lay. Go back to the beginning. Find out more about Pierre Rubidaux and spend less time swinging away at Gulfland. But time was a speeding enemy. In less than thirty-six hours, the money would be in Bouchet's hands and all hell would break lose when the worthless paper flooded the market. Damn the man for dying! For bringing on his own death by talking too much to too many people in too many places, and being overheard, no doubt, on Bouchet's bugging devices.

Take it easy. Go back over everything about Pierre Rubidaux. Make the pieces fit even if they're rammed into place. He received the bills in payment for several shrimp catches. Bouchet must have decided to run a test on the product, see if it would pass or not. With only a few out, he could always claim ignorance, make up for the bad money out of his pocket and get off free. Something about them had caught the old man's attention. Then, when Bouchet himself had asked that the bills be returned, it made Rubidaux suspicious enough to have them checked. He had taken them to a photographer friend. The photographer had found something technical, that Pierre had been unable to understand well enough to explain in his letter. But why go to a photographer, and who was he? Why hadn't he come forward when Pierre was murdered? Afraid ... of whom? Neither Angelique nor Gaston Reevé knew any friend the dead man had known who was a photographer—even as a hobby. Dead end. So, unless he could get straight answers to direct questions from someone on the inside at Gulfland—and there didn't seem to be any chance of that considering the security arrangements now in force—he would have to do it the hard way. Retrace Pierre's activities over the past few weeks, where he went, who he saw, talked to. Hell, it was all work the police were better set up to handle. Dull, plodding, detail stuff that wasted manpower and took too much time.

A movement near the end of the block caught the Penetrator's attention.

A man stood at the corner, arrested in the process of turning to walk away. He had stopped, though, staring directly back at the doorway in which the Penetrator kept watch. He was wearing a suit, his hair neatly styled and from that distance he appeared to be about twenty-one. The Penetrator had not noticed any Gulfland security people outside the fence before, but it was entirely possible they were enlarging their patrol area to cover all possible routes of approach. They were sure scraping the bottom, though. This one was poorly trained, still looking directly at the spot that had attracted his attention, and taking a couple of hesitant steps toward it. This was all Mark needed, to be trapped between the swarm of guards and dogs beyond the twelve-foot chain-link fence and some eager beaver on his first job. Sure enough, the kid was going to earn his pay today. He reached under his coat, producing a small walkie-talkie. Extending the antenna, he spoke a few words.

Mark looked around to gauge how much time he had and if any holes were left unplugged. Only a few seconds passed before another one—made on the same assembly line—showed up at the opposite end of the block. He keyed his hand radio and a howl erupted from the one carried by the observant kid who'd summoned him. They yacked back and forth a few seconds, then began to walk toward each other, intent on the Penetrator's refuge.

Mark had selected this particular doorway because the building that contained it was on an alley. He had few options left. The Penetrator decided on a surprise move and to hell with the possibility they

108

had a trap rigged in the alley. He stepped out into full view on the stoop.

Confused by this event, the reserve who had been called up stopped, uncertain what to do next. They were close enough to have communicated in a voice hardly louder than a conversational tone, yet his radio crackled and the one in charge told him to keep moving.

Thrusting both hands in his pockets, whistling tunelessly, Mark started down the steps. Turning right, he began to saunter down the block like a guy without a care in the world.

"There's an alley there, Lenny," crackled over the walkie-talkie. "Keep an eye on it."

"I can see it, Paul," Lenny told the eager beaver.

Mark increased his pace until he was running the last few steps, darting around the building's end into dark shade in the alley. He drew his .45, thumb snicking off the safety, cocked and now unlocked, its eight rounds of mortician's helpers ready to bring more grief to Gulfland's security force. He was ready for them if they proved as inexperienced as they seemed, by following him into the alley. All he had to do was wait. . . .

Chapter 12

DIVERSIONARY FORCE

They were even greener than he thought, charging into the alley side by side, their hands empty, apparently unarmed.

Before their eyes adjusted to the change in light, the Penetrator stepped out, facing toward them, his Colt Commander held almost casually in one hand. But the nearly half-inch hole in its ugly muzzle was lined up exactly with the center of Paul's tie. Mark's words were spoken softly, but carried authority.

"Stop there. Hands behind your heads. Now lace the fingers and hold on tight."

Eyes filled with the sewer-pipe-sized barrel of his .45, they obeyed promptly without saying a word. The Penetrator walked closer.

"Now face that wall. Take two steps forward. Good. Spread your legs. Hands over heads." He came in close then and shoved them against the wall in the classic shakedown position. Quickly he patted them over for weapons. To his surprise they had none. The search over, one of the pair started to come to his feet. Mark stuck the muzzle of his .45 into his ear. Hard.

"Hey! Cool it! You the New Orleans pig, man?" Lenny asked.

"Nope."

"Are you Gulfland gestapo?"

"What if I am?" This was getting interesting. The fact that they were unarmed indicated to the Penetrator that they weren't working for Bouchet. Now he was anxious to find out what their game was.

"Then you better let us go, man," Paul began. "We got a right to be here. We have a parade permit says we can hold a protest demonstration. You rough us up and we'll go to the police."

"That's the way it is with you punks, isn't it?" Mark snapped. "When everything's going your way it's 'pigs.' But whenever things get rough, or some guy gets fed up with you animals pissin' on his lawn and punches one of you in the mouth, it's, 'Oh, please Mister Policeman, sir, help us. Our rights have been violated.' Shit! But you can stand up now, kiddies," Mark said in a different, bantering tone. "The nice man's not going to blow your brains out today. You can have your demonstration on schedule, because I don't give a damn if you have a dozen. I haven't any more use for Gulfland than you do."

They took hesitant, shuffling steps forward, taking their hands from the wall as they regained balance, turned to face the man behind them. Paul's face was mobile, a calculating glint in his eye.

"Say, if you're not with the pigs and you're not workin' for Gulfland, it wouldn't happen to be that you're that heavy dude who wiped out their super-polluter, would it?"

"If I was, would you expect me to tell you all about it?" the Penetrator replied. "But right now, I'm asking the questions. Who are you two?"

They got another look at his big blaster. He'd let them stand up, but hadn't put it away. The eager one forced a smile. "Peace, brother. I promise, no

111

more pointed questions. I'm Paul Nelson and this is Lenny Golden. We're the Green Earth People. At least we're crowd-control monitors for a Green Earth demonstration."

"That's right," his partner added.

"We were gonna have it Wednesday, after Mardi Gras was over, but that ship getting sunk was too good to pass up."

"Like why should that Penetrator dude get all the good publicity?" Lenny filled in. As he spoke, his eyes wouldn't meet those of the big man with the gun. "Right now, Gulfland is big news. We thought that if we demonstrated now, we'd get better coverage, you know, of our message."

"And what would that be?"

Paul got into the conversation once more, "That Gulfland, and everyone else who's talking about sea farming is wrong. *Raising* kelp and plankton for harvest will choke the waters, change the shape of the bottom, and alter currents. Along with massive catches of fish and all the outfall pollution from industries, it's going to destroy all life in the sea and then we're doomed."

"Besides," his partner took up the line, "when the source, processing, and distribution are all controlled by a single organization like Gulfland the price of the product will rise so high only the rich can afford it. It's just another capitalist plot to oppress and enslave the working class."

"With common laborers—ditch diggers—getting over five bucks an hour, I won't debate the fallacy of that argument," the Penetrator told them. To the eager one, he asked, "When's this demonstration supposed to start, Paul?"

Paul glanced at his watch. "About an hour from now. Why?"

112

An idea was forming rapidly for the Penetrator. Maybe he *could* get one more swing at Bouchet. A chance to dig out the missing pieces before he had to resort to doing it the hard way. "I thought I might join you."

"Well, ah," the Green Earth leader licked his lips, nervously eyeing Mark's .45. "We, uh, we don't allow any of our members to carry guns. We're, ah, non-violent."

Returning his weapon to its belt-clip holster, the Penetrator said accusingly, "You seemed ready enough for violence when you thought I was outnumbered two to one." He received a pair of sickly grins in reply.

"*Touché,*" Paul said. He took a deep breath, expelled part of it in a nervous sigh. "Well. Mister, ah, whoever you are, you've just joined a demonstration. Be at the corner of Felicity and Rousseau in half an hour. Bring some Mardi Gras stuff. Mask, costume. Things like that."

Over two hundred people had turned out for the Green Earth demonstration, the Penetrator estimated as he joined the crowd.

Many wore full costumes, contrasting patterns of black and white, red and yellow. Others were partially costumed and all wore masks. The Penetrator looked right at home among them. He had selected a garish exaggeration of a Napoleonic Dragoon officer's tunic and a devil mask. The masks and bits of costume—easy to remove in a hurry—would make identification difficult in the event of police intervention.

Here and there, among the demonstrators, he spotted the gold crescent and star of the New Orleans Department of Police, worn as lapel pins or tie tacks by plainclothes officers who were conferring with group leaders and verifying the route of march. Mark rejected a placard on a tall pole, accepting instead a large handful of leaflets. He started working his way toward the head of the roughly formed column.

There was more order in this chaotic milling than appeared on the outside. Monitors were everywhere with their walkie-talkies, gathering people into groups, forming a line. The Penetrator had just reached his chosen spot when they moved out.

Crossing the five-way intersection, they entered Religious Street. Rattling and pounding tamborines, thumping on bongo drums, and chanting, they marched the short block to Celeste, turning right and heading toward the wharf. A sparse crowd had gathered to line the sidewalks, thinking it was another Mardi Gras celebration. Mark Hardin worked his way farther to the front and to an outside edge, passing out leaflets to the spectators.

"Never more! Never more!" chanted the marchers.

"Save our seas! Save our seas!" came the descant reply from farther back.

Victory at Sea! declared one placard. There were many of the inevitable *Ecology Now!* signs and once clever *Sauvez la Mer.* Handing out leaflets, capering from one side of the street to the other, the Penetrator created the impression he was one of the leaders, while he studied the demonstrators from behind the anonymity of his mask.

There was the usual collection of longhairs, he saw, some grubby, some clean. As Lieutenant Santini had said, there was a sprinkling of older people and some robust health faddists. The bulk of them, though, like Paul Nelson and his pal, seemed to be serious young students, with a scattering of slightly radical college instructor types. Halfhearted applause came from a cross-section of spectators as they moved along.

Their goal—the big front gates of Gulfland Fishermen's Co-op—was reached without incident. The marchers formed an oval picket line, long and narrow, parading with their placards and banners, chanting their slogans. Crates and apple boxes appeared, forming a makeshift speaker's platform. A young man jumped on top of them, carrying a bullhorn.

He exhorted the demonstrators on to greater effort, then turned his back on them, directing his words toward Gulfland. "Your days are numbered," his amplified voice bellowed off the office building. "Give up your crimes against humanity while you can. We are not alone. Others know you for what you are. Last night was only a sample. Stop your rape of the seas! The will of the people can not be denied!"

"Power to the people! Power to the people!" the pickets chanted.

Ariflex motors whirred as TV cameramen exposed hundreds of feet of color film, panning from the picket line to the young speaker and on to the fence of Gulfland.

Twenty security men had rushed to back up the gate guards. They stood in a ragged line, wearing motorcycle helmets and carrying lengths of heavy metal-reinforced steam hose. Glowering through the chain-link fence at their taunters, they hefted their weapons eagerly. Jibes and insults rose from the demonstrators. Lacking the discipline of properly trained police officers, the security force soon joined in, hurling their own insults.

"Get a job, ya fuckin' bum!" one of the guards yelled.

"Yer mother barks at the mailman," one picket replied.

"Wha' did *yer* mother do with the baby? You look like the afterbirth," another Gulfland goon quipped.

"Soo-o-o-oee! Pig, pig, pig, pig!" a hog caller among the Green Earth People gave out.

"Go-o-o fuck yourselves!" three security types chorused.

There was an angry mutter among the demonstrators. Many women and children were with them. Mark Hardin moved among them, urgently whispering a suggestion. Wherever he had passed, a new chant sprang up, growing in volume as others joined, repeating it over and over. It was a revised version of the blood-chilling, barbaric incantation from the mouths of small boys in Golding's *Lord of the Flies.*

"Kill the pig! Cut his throat! Spill his blood!"

Things were getting out of hand. The young speaker climbed down, handing the bullhorn to another group leader who took his place on the platform. "Hey, gang! Hey! This is a peaceful demonstration. Remember what we're here for. Save our seas! Save our seas! Come on now, save our seas!"

"Kill the pig! Kill the pig!" they replied.

"Hey, gang!" His voice cracked with nervous excitement. This was all going wrong. He had to stop them. "Hey, gang! Remember, the corrupt forces of the capitalist oppressors will crumble from internal rot. *Please,*" he begged, "keep it non-violent. Save our seas! Never more! Save our seas!"

But they weren't listening to dialectic today. *"Spill his blood! Spill his blood!"*

We're in deep shit, the young organizer realized as he looked around wildly for someone who could regain control of the demonstrators who had so quickly turned into a mob. And there he was! A great big guy standing at the edge of the platform, calm as if nothing was happening, reaching for the loudhailer. He recognized his rescuer now, that devil mask and weird coat. He'd seen devil mask as the head of the march, leading. He must have some authority. He was glad to hand it—and the responsibility—off to the big man, relinquishing his place on the stand.

"Green Earth People! Listen up!" the Penetrator's voice boomed over the chanting. He'd never started a riot before, but long ago—in another place and another life—as Sergeant Mark Hardin, U.S. Army, he had learned the key phrases by which you could recognize mob leaders. That was when they were still teaching classes on riot control, back when rioting and looting were crimes, punished by troops in the streets.

At least *this* riot, he offered himself as an excuse, was for a good cause. No one would get seriously hurt with those rubber truncheons and it would provide a good diversion. "Send the women and children to the rear!" As they quieted and complied, he went on, "Last night was just the beginning. Whoever did it showed us the way. We have the power to end their pollution forever. Charge the fence! Power to the people!"

With a savage roar, the mob hit the gates. Chain links held a moment, then bulged inward, the pipe frames parting under continuous pressure and forming a gap. Security men converged, truncheons flailing, but the gates widened and angry demonstrators streamed through.

"We don't have enough trouble, we have to have a gawdamned riot!" Anton Colbert bellowed at the guard commander who brought him word of the gates being forced by angry demonstrators.

"Where's those goddamned bimbos we hired as guards? Get 'em down there! Every one of them!" The unfortunate guard captain rushed out to relay his boss's orders.

Jes-us H. Christ! First it's this Penetrator shootin' our boys full of holes, guttin' 'em, shippin' bodies back to us. Then sinkin' our canner. Now a fuckin' riot. Could he be behind this, too? Bullshit! No guy's good enough to blow up a ship at three A.M. and then organize a full-scale riot by noon the next day. Then again, you never know.

"Hey!" Colbert yelled after the retreating guard. "I'm comin' with you."

Downstairs, out on the yard, it was a madhouse. Guards were thumping heads with their steam hose billys and being thumped back with whatever the rioters could find. A shower of broken brick, rocks, and bottles fell on the defenders. Two men went down.

Good thing I come down to take charge, Colbert thought. "George, Ted, get the fire hoses," he commanded aloud. "Knock them punks on their asses. That's the way to do it." There's a bunch'a creeps usin' sign poles like spears. All a gang of spearchuckin' monkeys, truth to tell.

"Hal," one guard hollered from the milling, struggling force at the gates. "You see that big guy? The one leadin' them?"

"Naw," the other shouted back. "Didn't you get him?"

"Hell, no. Hey, guys, keep an eye open for that big mean-lookin' dude leadin' these creeps!" he shouted to the others.

His words got through to his boss standing back by

the office building. *Big, mean-lookin' dude!* Hell, it couldn't be. That's what P.K. had called that Penetrator bastard. Nobody could get his shit together that fast. The Penetrator on the loose inside here? Bullshit! Never happen. Better check though. Who's that? He's packin' a rod. Must be one of the new men; them punks don't carry heat. He's big enough to turn over a tank, though. Get him to come along. If that Penetrator sonofabitch is here, sic that monster on him an' see how far he goes. Good, he caught my signal. Now we'll get that bastard.

"Let's go, Colbert," the Penetrator said as he walked up to Gulfland's security chief, prodding Colbert in the chest with his .45 Commander.

Anton Colbert blinked. His face washed clear of expression, the mind behind it dumped from its rails. It couldn't be him! Hell, it's one of our guys. I just called him over, right? Then he looked into the large black hole of the Colt's automatic pistol, down the valley of death and, for an instant, thought he saw the heavy bullet poised at the other end, anxious to tear into flesh, smash bone, and crush out life ... his flesh, his bone, his life. His mouth fell open, throat working a second before the voice came through. "Ohmygod!"

Without resistance, Anton Colbert turned and walked away, ahead of the Penetrator, angling between the office building and processing plant, toward a secondary dock. It was surprising how clear his mind could function now. There was an old net shed on that unused dock, not used now for some ten years. The Penetrator was taking him there. He was going to die and there was nothing he could do to stop it from happening.

"Hey, boss, where you goin'?" called a security man from behind them.

And it seemed only natural for the Penetrator to answer him, "We think we found that big guy. Stay there and handle that mob; we'll take care of it."

Inside the net loft Anton Colbert was brought back to reality by a backhand slap to the head. It knocked him to his knees nearly unconscious, because the hand was filled with a Colt Commander.

"Time to tell it all, Colbert," the Penetrator said as he lifted the smaller man to his feet. "You can do it the easy way—just answer questions—and live to walk out of here. Or make it hard and I'll use a needle on you. Under the babble juice you'll spill your guts and wind up dead."

Colbert rallied his cowering spirit, "You can't get away with this for long, you know. The cops are looking for you, too. You don't have a chance."

A big, hard fist buried itself deep in Colbert's gut, driving the wind from him and bringing tears of pain to his eyes. The Penetrator's Colt had gone back under his coat, leaving both hands free to work. "I've heard that other places. Try me on something new. Pierre Rubidaux. Fill me in on that one."

"Piss on you. All I have to do is shout and ..." and he stopped talking, hands grasping his jaw like a man with a toothache. The Penetrator had darted two hooked fingers to the side of his victim's jaw, curling over the bone from behind and mashing the nerve trunk against it.

"Can't talk yet?" Mark taunted. "I'll finish it for you. All you have to do is shout and die. You're not a big security man any more and you're going to get littler before I get through with you, if you don't answer up. Let's try Rubidaux again."

It hurt like hell! Anton Colbert glared at the Penetrator with impotent hatred. When he finally spoke,

120

the words were fuzzy, "I' wassn' me. Din know bat it. P.K. did't."

Pow! The Penetrator flashed two cupped hands to the sides of Colbert's head, boxing his ears. Such a blow could permanently deafen a man, burst his eardrums, and leave him forever in a world of silence. It had been carefully calculated to come just short of that point. But the blood running from one of Colbert's ears indicated he had lost at least half of his hearing. He had sunk to his knees, doubled over with incredible pain, twisting his head from side to side in agony, hands held helplessly over his ears. The Penetrator kicked him in the ribs, flattening him out backward onto the floor of rough dock timbers. Then he stepped forward, straddling the other man. "Now," Mark demanded, raising his voice to be sure he was heard. "Pierre Rubidaux. Tell it all."

It all came then. Pierre Rubidaux had discovered something wrong with the counterfeit money. A flaw that would tip off the Feds. They had heard him talking about it on the listening devices in his house and at Gaston Reevé's. They learned, too, that he had written to someone called the Penetrator, but that meant nothing at the time. Peter Keoh and Anton Colbert had been the "fishermen" witnesses. Carlo Santini was in on the money deal, so that part was easy. Colbert and Keoh had caught Rubidaux on his boat Friday morning and jammed the marlin spike in his chest. They had left him to die where he fell. Neither Colbert nor Peter Keoh knew then that Angelique had gone out on the boat the night before and was sleeping below. The struggle must have awakened her. She was on deck with her father when the local police arrived. She accused Gulfland and Bouchet of engineering her father's death. San-

121

tini's "investigation" had smoothed that over. But Marcel Bouchet was convinced that the old man had lived long enough to tell his daughter what had happened and something about the evidence he had collected. Perhaps, Bouchet believed, she even knew where he had hidden it. It was a disappointing yield. Other than the gang version of Rubidaux's murder, there was nothing new in what Colbert said.

Walking away from Anton Colbert's prone figure, the Penetrator searched the old shed for a suitable piece of material. All he could find was a large coil of old lead line, used to weight the bottoms of fish nets. It was dusty and stiff, but it would do. Slowly it began to take form.

He had just finished the thirteenth loop when he returned to Colbert's side. The Gulfland security boss had managed to sit up. When he saw what the Penetrator held in his hands, his eyes rolled wildly and his voice grated with terror as he begged. "No! Oh, no! For the love of God, no! You promised . . ."

"Sometimes I lie a lot."

Colbert rose unsteadily to his feet. "There's more. I . . . I . . . I can tell you all of it. Just don't . . . don't do that."

"Give."

"They're . . . going after the girl. Today at her father's funeral. P.K. and four others. Bouchet said to kill her right on the spot. I swear it. I told you, right? Dear God in Heaven, don't use that thing."

"They used to hang people for murder in this state," the Penetrator told the terrified Colbert as he tossed the loose end of the lead line over a beam. He fitted the noose over Colbert's head. "I guess that's good enough for you."

Anton Colbert's knees gave way, his body sagging

against the grim executioner who stood before him, clutching at the Penetrator's coat. "Oh, Jesus. Oh, God no! Please not this way. Oh, sweet God . . ."

His words were choked off as the Penetrator hauled on the free end of the line, drawing Colbert off his feet. Stepping to one side, the Penetrator secured the lead line to a deck cleat screwed into one wall for net draping. Anton Colbert clawed at the braided nylon loop that slowly strangled the life out of him.

Colbert's struggles slackened and stopped, his face purpled, tongue protruding and arms slack at his sides. The Penetrator walked over to the dangling Colbert. He placed an arrowhead in the dead man's shirt pocket. Crossing to the door, he opened it and started out . . . then stopped, rigid. Even his breathing suspended.

He was facing the thick muzzle of a silenced .380 Beretta. . . .

Chapter 13

FUNERAL FOR FOUR

On the working end of the graceful little pistol with its ugly snout was the pockmarked gunman, hired by Wo Fat Ling's henchman to bring the Penetrator in alive.

His lips split open, revealing overly large, yellow teeth.

"Nice and easy, sweetheart. Keep both them hands in sight. Now, yer comin' with me, real peaceful like."

"I'm sorry, but I can't do that. I have another engagement. I'm going to a funeral," the Penetrator told him, left arm flashing out, stiff-arming the surprised gunman, as his right hand groped in his coat pocket for the Hi-Standard derringer.

Sowers' Beretta coughed softly, the bullet gouging a deep, painful trough in the flesh of Mark's right side. The Penetrator gave an involuntary cry as he jerked the palm gun free of his coat, blasting both barrels into Sowers' face. The pair of twenty-two mag super stoppers jellied his brain and he fell backward onto the dock planks before he could trigger another shot.

Mark was bleeding like a throat-slashed stag. It was only a grazing wound, slicing him open, rather than puncturing a hole through the skin, but a serious one. He used a clean handkerchief and his belt to temporarily cut off the flow of blood and began to look around the dock.

Even without the weakening wound and its tell-tale crimson splashes on his side, he would never be able to walk out. The mini-riot he had started was still in progress from the sounds that reached him and, busy as they were, the guards were sure to spot him. He found something that would serve. A small, flat-bottomed boat was tied up to the dock. Checking the area around him for any prying observers, Mark jumped down into the boat, casting off. Surprisingly, the little ten-horse kicker was warm. It caught on the first pull of the cord and the Penetrator threw it in gear, purring quickly away from Gulf-land's dock.

Behind him, on the dock, the Chinese stepped out from around one corner of the net shed. He cursed the Penetrator with deep feeling and impotent frustration. He vowed to get revenge, to exact his own vengeance before turning the Penetrator over to Wo Fat Ling. It was a personal thing now, a matter of face. He had other reasons. His hired gunman, Sowers, highly recommended as the best one around to do the job, lay dead at his feet. A riot was in progress behind him and he had no way out. That putrid Occidental scum, thrice-cursed spawn of the many-horned devil, the Penetrator, was calmly putting away from the dock in *his* boat! The same skiff the two of them had used to get to their quarry when he had been spotted leading Anton Colbert to the shed. Snatching up the silenced Beretta, he ran along the dock, firing wildly at the retreating form in the small boat.

Back at his car—Mark was still driving the dark blue Buick he had taken from his would-be ambushers—the Penetrator cleaned his wound. He then used an antiseptic plastic spray bandage to cover it, finishing with a GI field dressing. Replacements for his clothes had to wait until he returned to his motel.

Uncomfortable in a dark suit, an off-the-rack job purchased for the occasion from a men's store near the Holiday Inn, he drove to Grand Isle for Pierre Rubidaux's funeral. It was to be a requiem mass at Our Lady of Lourdes Church and Mark barely made it on time.

Religion had not been a part of Mark Hardin's life for more years than he could remember. And his brief career as the Penetrator held little that he believed fit subject matter for the confessional. Yet the habits of childhood controlled his actions as he entered the church. His fingers dipped into the holy water font, forming the sign of the cross as he genuflected in the aisle and slid into a pew.

"Dominus vobiscum," the priest concluded. Even the most hardened apostate could be moved by the solemn dignity of the mass for the dead. Mercifully, it was a short service and now the people were outside, making ready for the drive to the cemetery and graveside service.

So far there had been no sign of any of the Gulfland hoods the Penetrator knew on sight, nor anyone who looked out of place or acted strangely. A brief word with Gaston Reevé arranged that Mark's car would follow immediately behind the family car, giving him a close view of anything out of the ordinary. When the stately decorum of the church was handed over temporarily to the oily obsequiousness of the soft-handed funeral director, Mark went for his car, slipping a few items from the trunk into his pockets before driving into line.

Mark was becoming tense, worried over the lack

of overt action he had been expecting. Nothing had gone wrong on the three-mile course taken by the cortege. Now, at the cemetery, out in the open, the hazards were greatly increased. As Mark climbed from his car, eyes alert for an ambush, he winced from the burning gash in his side.

Angelique turned from the priest toward him. "You're hurt," she said, laying a hand on his arm, concern for his wellbeing momentarily wiping out her grief.

"It's nothing. I got shot this morning. It's really just a nick. Hurts about as much as a sunburn," he lied. "We'll talk about it later. Don't worry. Let's do the rest of this properly."

She gave him a weak half-smile and returned to her place behind the priest. The pallbearers, led by Gaston, lifted the coffin and started toward the canopy covering the open grave. Behind them walked the priest, followed by three small altar boys. Angelique Rubidaux came next, the principal mourners ranking behind her. Mark stood aside, watching the procession form and keeping an eye on the cemetery in general. The many old-fashioned crypts and the broad bowls of cypress trees provided too many inviting spots for a sniper. None of this was to his liking at all. If there had been any way to keep Angelique from this spot, he would have done so. But proper respect must be shown the dead and neither Angelique nor Gaston would consent to a change. When the last of the mourners started off, he joined the procession.

Halfway to the grave, he spotted them. Four strange men, standing off to one side near an open crypt. The bulges under their armpits and their hard faces left no doubt that they were the ones. Peter Keoh must be acting as wheel man. Plastering an undertaker's professional smile on his face, the Penetrator left the rear of the file, walking directly toward them. His left hand was in his coat pocket.

"Good afternoon, gentlemen. Are you friends of the deceased?"

Before they could react, frame an answer to the Penetrator's question, they found themselves looking down the muzzle of his .45 Colt Commander. Mark's body blocked his actions from view by those around the grave, but he had to make this fast. He looked around.

A pile of tools sat in a wheelbarrow beside the open door of the tomb. The caretaker must be off on a lunch break. Whatever, it would have to do. "Over there," he commanded, pointing with his chin, Indian fashion, their eyes following his direction. They hesitated, then saw his finger tightening on the trigger and walked to the crypt. "Inside," he ordered.

As the last gunsel entered, the Penetrator took his left hand from his pocket. He held an old-style M-3 fragmentation grenade. The Penetrator turned away slightly so they could not see what he was doing. He slipped the middle finger of his right hand through the grenade's safety ring and pulled it out, dropping it outside the crypt. Thrusting his left hand into the doorway, he ordered the last gunman, "Here, hold this."

Automatic reflex compelled the other man to reach out, taking the deadly object before he realized what it was. Then the Penetrator slammed the door, locking it! Clutching an armed grenade, trapped in a barred and windowless room, there was nothing any of them could do, except be very, very careful.

By that time, the Penetrator had moved away, joining the others at the grave. Father Baudreau was just finishing, making the sign of the cross over the coffin with a gold crucifix.

"*Requiescat in pace,*" he intoned.

Then everyone was back in the cars, driving out of the cemetery. Near the edge of the grounds, Mark spotted P.K., sitting in his car, waiting for his boys. And just then, Mark could swear he felt a slight thump of air displacement and a light ground shock as the grenade detonated. Oh, well, you win a few and lose a few. "Better luck next time, boys." He laughed aloud.

After eating in a nearby restaurant, the Reevé family were taken back to their hotel. Mark, Gaston, and at Mark's request, Jiggs Flobert, Bobby Reevé, and Angelique drove on to Grand Isle, to the dock where the *Christy Sue* was tied up. They paused a few minutes while Mark admired the blue-and-white craft sitting lightly in the water. Gaston was filled with pride.

"Eh! You like her, no? Fastest boat in the Gulf. Thirty-four feet, only draws six-eight inches of water unloaded. Those twin motors give her plenty speed, I tell you. I build her up myself, me and Jiggs. *Christy Sue* . . . she's not the biggest, but we sure think she's the best."

"She's a real beauty, Gaston," Mark told him truthfully. "How big a crew you use?"

"She sleeps four, but I only use one man besides Jiggs here. I swear he's in love with those Mercurys. Makes them purr like a pussycat."

At Mark's suggestion, they entered Gaston's net shed, finding seats where they could. Mark paced the floor, trying to frame the right words.

"I suggested we come here because we won't be interrupted and the place isn't bugged. I'm sure now

129

that the only way to bring this all to an end is to go over everything Pierre said and did for the past few weeks. You four should know most of it. He's bound to have left a hint that will give us a lead. Angelique," he said, turning to the girl. "There is no doubt now that Bouchet wants you dead because he is convinced you know where your father hid the evidence against them."

"But I don't," she interrupted, protesting. "I've already told you everything."

"I know. This is pretty rough on you, but let's go over it all again. From the time he told you that he'd written to me. Any word, a hint, a phrase that might remind you of where he hid ... whatever it was he had."

Angelique's head sank, large tears running down her cheeks. "He ... he never ... even ... named the ... ones who killed him. All he did was talk about the ... the old times." The tight control she had kept through the funeral gave way and she sobbed hoarsely, her whole body shaking.

Mark started to pace the floor again, helpless in the face of feminine grief. He went back over every alternative, finding no other way. She had to know something of importance to Bouchet and, hard as it was to do so, he had to get it from her. He stopped the pacing in front of her, shouting at her, forcing his voice to sound harsh with anger and contempt. "Stop that nonsense! This is more important than you or your father, any of us! If Bouchet gets away with this, the whole country's economy could collapse. And you sit there bawling like some goddamned three-year-old who's lost her candy. Grow up long enough to be some help."

She rocked with each of his words as if they were closed-fist blows to her body. Gulping and hiccoughing, Angelique controlled her tears. Gaston was half out of his chair, but a curt nod and wink from Mark, seen only by Gaston, sat him down. Angelique looked up, dry-eyed. A light died in her eyes, a light that had been there since the night they had spent together fighting his fever and finding love.

It's an awe-filled moment when love first dies. A burning, gut-wrenching, pitiful instant of emptiness and irrecoverable loss. It was worse than most, as Angelique's love for Mark died before his eyes. She changed as he watched, part of her fleeing, taking with it that essence of innocence that had been so like Donna Morgan. Mark felt it as intensely as she did, punishing him like a physical blow. Angelique! his mind cried out. My dearest Angelique, forgive me, my darling. He struggled to keep from reaching out to her, offering comfort, and his teeth clenched to keep from begging forgiveness. She shook her head negatively and began to speak in a monotone, a whipped child reciting a dreaded lesson.

"He talked about me, us, when I was little. He said it was Gulfland men who killed him, but didn't name them. He said to be careful, they might try to get me too. He said the evidence was hidden and no one would know where. He told me he loved me. He said to pray for him. He died."

Made nervous by an intensity of adult emotions he had never experienced before, and embarrassed by his inability to handle it all, Bobby Reevé began to hum a tune. Mark felt a burning in his eyes. He turned to the boy, brushing at the wetness on his face. "That song? They played it in the cemetery. At Pierre's funeral. What is it?"

Awed by the sight of tears on the big man's face, Bobby quit humming, unable to answer.

"It was his favorite song," Gaston told Mark.

"He used to tease me when I was little," Angelique continued in her toneless, defeated voice. "He would say that I was named after it. He ... he even hummed a little bit of it just before he died. He asked me if I remembered it and said I should never forget it. That ... that it would be very important to me."

"But what's its name?" Mark was numb. He was stunned by the impossibility of the suspicion growing on him. It couldn't be. It was a TV drama answer, yet ... it just might be.

"*Bayou Angelique,*" Bobby had found his voice again.

Impossible! But hope and time were running out. "I think," Mark stammered, "I think ... I know ... where Pierre hid his proof."

Chapter 14

BAYOU ANGELIQUE

They looked at Mark incredulously, then with growing hope. Everyone began to talk at the same time.

"What are the words to that song?" Mark raised his voice to be heard. The others quieted. "This sounds crazy, but I think Pierre meant this Bayou Angelique as a clue."

"*La lune est claire, mon petit amour,*" Gaston recited.

"In English," Mark said.

"Eh! It is easier to tell than to give the words. It is about a young man, a shrimper, who loves a pretty girl. He sings about the bright moon and his little love. This girl lives alone on the edge of a small lake in one bayou; the water is clear like her face and tiny like her body and he sees her every time he's not shrimping. Then, like most of these Cajun love songs, it turns sad. The girl gets sick—today we'd say malaria—and he finds her dead. He buries her beside her lake and remembers forever." Gaston finished. "Not much help, eh?"

"It isn't exactly what I was looking for. Is there such a place as Bayou Angelique?" Mark asked, fishing for anything to support his theory.

"Yes, there is."

"And Daddy used to take me there when I was little."

"That makes it look a little better," Mark said. "Anything else about it you can think of?"

"There *is* a little shack there, just like the song. And the water is clear—not so much nowadays, but better than most," Angelique recalled, the excitement of this prospect lifting her out of her earlier depression.

"It's worth a try. Where is this place?"

"North of here," Gaston told him. "Up Barataria Bay. It is near the place they say Jean Lafitte and his pirates hid out."

"A real treasure hunt. Wow!" Bobby joined in.

"They say that when you have eliminated every possible answer, try the impossible," Mark said. "How long would it take us to get there?"

"We'll have to go by boat," Angelique answered.

"Close to two hours on the *Christy Sue*," Gaston supplied. "Jiggs . . ."

"I'll help Jiggs get the *Christy* ready," Bobby volunteered. "Then we can leave sooner."

"You're not going, son," Gaston told his boy. "Bouchet may have men watching our boat. Too much danger if they're around."

Disappointment was plain to read on Bobby's face. The thrill of adventure, a search for hidden clues, was a big thing in his young life. He looked from his father to Mark Hardin, his lips silently framing a question, "Fred?" Mark shook his head negatively. The excitement that shone in the boy's eyes misted over. Then he brightened suddenly. "I'll help Jiggs anyway. Then can I stay with Larry, Pop? Until you guys come back?"

"*Sacre nom!* You are a man already, son. Sure, you do that."

134

Only a few minutes passed before the twin sixty-horse inboard-outboard Mercurys on the *Christy Sue* were idling in a deep-throated rumble. Jiggs opened the door to the net shed. "She's ready. Let's go."

"The boy?" Gaston asked with parental concern.

Jiggs shrugged expansively. "Gone already. Couldn't stop talking about all the things he would tell his friends." He tossed an empty Jax can into one corner of the room. "No time to get more, eh?"

"I have to get something from the car," Mark told them. "I'll meet you on board." The Penetrator was troubled more than he let on to the others. The possibility that Reevé's boat was being watched was more than likely. Accordingly, he selected several items from the trunk and placed them in his attaché case, returning to the dock.

Angelique was waiting for him. Her eyes, filled with hurt and confusion, avoided his. Mark set down the briefcase, reaching out for her, holding her by the shoulders. She took a step backward, pulling free. Her voice was low, uncertain. "I . . . it's all . . . we . . . why?"

A thousand stones of loss and regret weighed down upon him. Mark wanted so much to reach out to her again, to touch her, hold her close and take back the harsh words he had so recently spoken. Angelique. Angelique. She was so small and perfect, so shining bright—truly angelic. Words came hard to him, harder than when he had shouted at her in mock anger. "Oh, Angel. I am sorry. So very sorry. I had to say something to bring you out of it. To get you talking again about what happened. Time is so short. And the mission . . ."

"The mission," her words were bitter, unforgiving. "You have to sacrifice everything for the *mission*. There's no room in you for anything but your

135

crusade to save the world. Everything has to go, the law, decency, honor ... love. When we made love, you called me by another name. Was that part of the mission, too?"

"What about revenge, Angelique? Don't you want to see your father's murderers pay for what they did? I hanged one today. Anton Colbert and the one they call P.K. killed your father. I made a noose out of lead line and lynched Colbert. Strung him up and watched him die."

Eyes wide with horror, lips twisted into an anguished slash, Angelique gulped back a sob. Then suddenly she was in Mark's arms, holding him tightly, her body writhing against his. "Oh, my darling," she cried. "I didn't ... you shouldn't have ... but it's ... oh, I need you."

But the light wasn't back. Would never come back. What they had shared was as dead as the long-dead Donna Morgan, and, like her, would only come back in dreams.

"Ho, you two!" Gaston Reevé called from the low-topped cabin of the *Christy Sue*. "Son-of-a-gun, you want to make love, you wait till the night, eh?"

His well-meaning good humor cut through the awkwardness of their situation. Retrieving his attaché case, Mark sprinted to the boat, Angelique holding on to his free hand. They jumped aboard just as Jiggs cast off the bow line. Gaston eased the throttles forward and spun the wheel, sending them away from the rickety dock in a gentle arc. Jiggs took his usual place, a high chair in the stern, between his spotless engines. He cocked his head from side to side, listening as Gaston increased power. Patting the big Mercs affectionately, he beamed with pride. They were skirting the western shore, working to make the best line through the bay. As their speed increased, the going got rougher.

There was a slight cross chop, driven by a stiff wind, and the bow slammed down on each roller. Each time it slapped the water, sheets of spray came over the bow, washing down the deck. Mark and Angelique were driven inside the cabin.

"We're making about twelve knots," Gaston estimated. "It's gonna be rough until we get up to speed."

"She'll go faster than this?" Mark asked.

"Our shallow draft," Gaston explained. "She acts a lot like a hydroplane. Light loaded like this, she'll make twenty-two, twenty-five knots, maybe more." He looked over his shoulder for Jiggs' approving nod, then shoved the throttles full forward, changing gears as his hand came away.

Christy Sue seemed to leap from under them. The stern settled down, screws digging in, sending a rooster-tail higher than the cabin. The bow rose high out of the water, planing across the waves. The sensation of speed was exhilarating. Mark found himself, like everyone else, grinning idiotically, the thrill of conquering the relentless sea capturing them all.

"Look," Jiggs shouted over the engine noise. "Over there to starboard." They turned to the right side portholes. "It's a Gulfland boat," Jiggs said.

Peering through the spray-streaked plexiglass opening, Mark located the other boat. It was painted red and white, flying a blue pennant with a white circle. In the circle was a red capital G. The Gulfland boat was running a parallel course to their own, keeping station pretty well, Mark thought, bow to midships.

"I was right. Those sonsabitches," Gaston swore. "They were keeping watch for *Christy Sue*. They don't have a chance, we outrun them easy, you'll see. Hey, Jiggs, you make out her name?"

Moving around the starboard engine, the little man peered intently at the other boat. "The *Ibis*, I think," he announced after due study.

Gaston laughed gustily. "Too bad, *Ibis*. *Christy Sue*, she eat you up on this water."

His prediction proved out as their greater speed widened the gap between their watchers and the little shrimp boat. Thanks to their shallow draft, they skirted close inshore to the many islands that dotted Barataria Bay, gaining more lead when the bigger boat could not follow them. As the *Christy Sue* bounded across open water, widening the gap with each second, Gaston swung the wheel hard to port and they entered Little Lake, zig-zagging between the twin islands at its mouth where it joined Barataria.

"Not far now," Gaston hollered. "Look, they aren't behind us any more. They don't know where we go. So, they have to look around the islands first. Sound gets muffled around here. Bouncing off these islands, you can't tell where it comes from. It's an old smuggler's trick."

They passed the Innercostal Waterway and were nearly to the entrance to Bayou Barataria before Gaston cut the throttles back and turned into a narrow water course. Jiggs came forward, picking up a long pole and standing ready in the bow. The narrow channel was nearly choked off with cypress knees and mangrove, great boughs of them closing off the sunlight. They entered cautiously, ghosting along at two knots. They had been on the water for an hour and a half and now time crept by as they passed through a maze of direction-losing scenery.

Jiggs fended off the banks as they rounded a

sharp bend and Mark thought the water looked clearer. Through a serpentine maze of switch-back bends and around another right-angle turn the water suddenly became a crystal lens, magnifying the sandy bottom. Bright sunlight caused them to blink as the cypress and mangrove widened away, following the opening shore line, leaving them in a small, clear lagoon. Gaston touched up the throttles slightly and the *Christy Sue* headed for the opposite shore. Over there, Mark could discern the vague outline of a decrepit shack.

"Okay, Jiggs, drop the hook." Gaston cut the throttles and put the gears in neutral as he spoke. An anchor—much too small for a boat this size, Mark thought—went over the side and caught, paying out the hemp anchor line. The bottom was shelving fast and as the line went taut, the boat pivoted on its stem, the stern gently grounding in the shallows. A reddish sand beach lay before them and, at the edge of the trees, a shack. A human voice would have shattered the illusion of this capsule paradise.

Silence. Insect hums and the cry of a distant heron. Then there was a muffled gagging sound coming from the fish well. Someone coughing and retching. Mark and Gaston reached it at the same time. Gaston threw open the lid, releasing a sheepish-looking Bobby Reevé.

"Robert!" his father thundered threateningly. "What the hell do you think you're doing, boy?"

"I just had to come along," his son pleaded. "I couldn't stay there and let you have all the fun." He tried to flash a smile, but paled a gray-green and looked as if he was going to be sick again. The kid was a mess, wet with oily bilge water, stained from head to bare feet with fish slime and vomit.

"You know better than to disobey, son. I'll fix you

good when we get home, warm your butt with my strap till you can't sit down." Gaston's anger began to crack into a grin as he studied his bedraggled son. "Son-of-a-gun. You're a stinkin' mess, boy. Over the side with you and clean up right away."

Bobby dived from the weather rail, striking the water flat and sending up a high wave. He swam out a few strokes and began to strip off his clothes, washing them a piece at a time, wadding them up and throwing them back on deck. When he was buck naked, he pulled away further, cleaned himself as much as possible and swam back to the boat. His nakedness did not embarrass him among these adults—growing up in a family of thirteen children left little room for false modesty—and he calmly began to dress as the others climbed over the side to go ashore.

"Well. Bayou Angelique," Gaston said. "Where do we begin?"

Mark studied the terrain. "The shack was in the song. So, we might as well begin with the obvious. Search in the walls, floor, under the floor, tear it apart if we have to."

"Hey you, stowaway," Gaston called to his son, turning toward the boat. "Now you're here, you might as well make yourself useful. Help us search." That took no second urging. Bobby let out a whoop and vaulted the rail, splashing up to them.

An hour later, they had exhausted every possibility around the shack. Everyone had worked up a good sweat, but zero results. Bobby looked longingly at the cool water.

"All right, everybody," Mark called them together. "What next? I'm positive that the song meant more than just the general location of his hiding place. I'm betting it gives the exact spot."

140

"I'm afraid not," Gaston said. "The song's all about fishing and their love and moonlight." Jiggs shook his head in agreement.

"No. Wait a minute," Angelique countered. "The next to the last verse. He finds his love dead of the fever and takes her out to bury her."

"Where?" Mark asked.

"Under a big cypress. How does it go? 'I lay my love 'neath the mighty cypress, its giant knees her resting place to guard.'"

"We'll try it," Mark declared. "Dig around the base of every large cypress here, if we have to."

At the third "mighty cypress" they found it. A large gallon jar, sealed with wax, containing an oil-skin-wrapped package and buried about ten inches underground. They all clustered around while Mark opened the packet. Inside were fifteen crisp new bills in denominations of twenty and fifty dollars, several photo enlargements of portions of the bills, and a long note in Pierre's handwriting. Mark read it through, then went back to read aloud for the others' benefit.

Pierre Rubidaux first noticed the bills, he explained in his letter, because he was a sometime coin collector. Not serious, but keeping an eye for the unusual. The first five bills were truly unusual, he said. They were crisp and new—in uncirculated condition. But they were old money, printed in 1934, while silver certificates were still in circulation. The tipoff to this was the legend to the left of the portraits. On these bills—what Pierre called *real money*, notes with something to back them up—it read that it was redeemable in *gold*. All bills of 20, 50, and 100 denomination read so until the new series of 1950. It would be unusual, after so many years, to find so many of these bills in uncirculated condition. The

141

thing that really caught his attention, though, was the color of ink used on the seal and serial numbers. It was all wrong. The bills had been printed using the same light, vivid green color for seals and serial numbers as was used on currency now in circulation from the Federal Reserve, instead of being yellow as it should be for series of 1934 notes. That could never be. These were the bills Bouchet had tried to buy back.

Then, a week later, Pierre received the other ten in payment for his catch. They appeared proper in every way, the legend to the left of the portrait reading simply, "This note is legal tender for all debts public and private," with no promise of anything to back up its value. Yet, there was something about them that seem "off" somehow. It was one of these he had sent to the Penetrator. Pierre had taken some of them to a friend who worked in photography. He had enlarged them and found flaws. His explanation was on the back of one picture.

Mark turned over the photograph and read aloud. "These bills are definitely counterfeit, Pierre. They were made on an offset press and the U.S. Government doesn't use offset.

"Offset presses use a diazo-coated metal plate, the image burned onto them from a photographic negative. The plate is very delicate, so it can't come in contact with the paper. Moving at high speed, the paper would quickly wear out the plate. So, ink is transferred—or offset—from the plate to a rubber blanket. This, in turn, is what makes the impression on the paper. Sometimes the blanket gets what is called in the trade a *ding*. A bit of dust, a hair, or a piece of paper indents the blanket so it doesn't offset the ink. Then something that should be printed isn't.

"That's what happened with your bills. In the

case of the twenty, it must have been a small piece of dust. In the enlargement you can see a double highlight in Jackson's right eye, giving him a slightly crosseyed look. On the fifty a hair or touch-up brush bristle caused what looks like a scar on Grant's lip. The same flaw appears on every bill you gave me of each denomination. The Treasury Department doesn't let mistakes like those slip past and get in circulation. True, the same sort of thing can and does happen on the letter presses at the Bureau of Printing and Engraving. But faulty bills are destroyed, then a new press run is made, reprinting them with the same serial number and the public is none the wiser.

"I hope this will help you. Sincerely, John."

There was no other name on the photo, but a large rubber stamp impression gave the name of a photography shop in New Orleans, along with its address and phone number. "That does it," Mark told them. "We have a case now. Tomorrow, two of you go to Baton Rouge, see the Attorney General and the Secret Service."

"Why not the office in New Orleans?"

"Too much chance of Bouchet's goons seeing you, Gaston. They'd shoot you down before you ever got there. While you're doing that, I'm going to take one more swing at Gulfland."

Mark was more than satisfied that they had all they needed. The information contained in Pierre Rubidaux's cache not only identified the errors in the counterfeit, but tied it to Bouchet and, with the letter Mark took from the safe, Bouchet and the counterfeit were tied directly to Cuba. The others had been passing Pierre's evidence around, looking at the photos. Now Mark gathered it up. "Time to get out of here. We'll have a lot to do tomorrow."

"Sonofabitch!" Gaston exclaimed. "There they come again."

"Can we outrun them, like last time?" Mark asked, hoping his limited knowledge of seamanship proved wrong.

"No, *mon ami,* there is more than speed involved on the water. They are coming toward us. Look there," he pointed off the port bow, to where the larger *Ibis* that had pursued them before was closing on them. "She can . . . how you say? . . . cross our *T.* Then we never escape."

"I thought only sailing ships were affected by that."

"Not so, my friend. Closing on us, she uses her speed *and* ours, and *Ibis* has seaway to maneuver while we have to turn inside her. She can come across our bow, making us throttle back or hit her, and then down one side, across the stern, and half-way up the other side before we can get away. Or she just lay dead in the water across our bow, hope we won't choose to ram her. They know me good, those Gulfland *bâtards.* That I would never do!"

Mark looked around, taking stock of their armament. He was in the worst possible predicament, trapped among four of the sheep while the wolves ravened only two hundred yards away. Outside of his .45 and the Hi-Standard derringer—both of which were useless at this range—there was only a .22 Ruger carbine equipped with a cheap 4X scope, Gaston's shark gun. Small help if it came to a fire fight, but some. Then there was the bundle of death in his attaché case. Effective up to three hundred meters, the present situation made it almost their only hope. Surrounded by civilians! It was a hell of a way to fight a war.

Angelique had to come along because of the song

144

and her familiarity with the bayou. Gaston and Jiggs? They'd seen it all, knew the risks, the odds. But a kid! He hardly looked eleven, let alone thirteen, and far too young to play the game with death.

Electing to risk a ramming, the Gulfland boat throttled back, drifting into the path of the *Christy Sue*. Gaston cut his speed even before two shots were fired aboard the *Ibis*, thudding into their bow. "Ah, the bastards," he swore as he cut speed even more. A voice came across the water, amplified by a bullhorn.

"Ahoy the *Christy Sue*. Captain Reevé, heave to and stand by to receive a boarding party. Do as I say or everyone aboard will die." His words were emphasized by another shot from the crow's nest of *Ibis*. It shattered the starboard running light.

"So. The big fish are out today. That's Phil DuBois. I recognize that high yellah *cochon*'s voice. Ah, what the hell. They kill us all anyway," Gaston said as he firewalled the throttles, spinning the wheel hard left and running parallel with the Gulfland boat's course, but in the opposite direction. "Make them work for it, eh?"

A volley of shots came from DuBois' craft, which was working hard to reverse course and get under way. Most shots went wide, but several thumped into the stern boards and fantail. They were still within pistol range, so Mark returned fire. But the up-and-down motion of the boat, combined with a slight sideways skewing of the stern as the screws dug in, threw his aim off enough that the enemy remained full strength and unharmed.

Jiggs knelt between his engines, checking their oil level and making minute adjustments, nursing the maximum power from them. Slowly they began to pull away from their pursuers. Peter Keoh was still firing his big bore rifle from the crow's nest. The bullets came through the open stern light, snapping past them and splintering wood from the cabin walls. Phil DuBois opened up from the bow with an automatic carbine. The thirty-caliber slugs sprayed the water around the *Christy Sue*. He corrected for increasing range and bullets spanged off the engine housings, showering them with metal fragments. Angelique cried out, grabbing her arm as blood ran from several small cuts. Jiggs suddenly uttered a strangled gasp, half rising from his place between the engines, a red stain spreading on chest and back. A lucky shot by Keoh caught him in the head, ripping out the back and spattering the others with blood and gray matter.

As thick blood and pulpy tissue splashed on her, Angelique screamed. She gagged and turned away, vomiting into the open bilge. Bobby propelled himself off the bunk where he had been lying out of the line of fire. He knelt on the deck, cradling the dead man's shoulders in his arms. The boy was dry-eyed, but sobbed hysterically, "Uncle Jiggs! Uncle Jiggs!" Gaston worked at the wheel, trying to angle his boat away from the *Ibis* so that the stern was no longer exposed to deadly fire. Mark was at the opposite bunk, digging in his briefcase, hurrying to put the heavy stuff into use before anyone else was hit.

Gaston shouted in pain and the wheel spun free as he fell to the deck, clutching his shoulder. It wasn't a serious hit, but he was out of the action. Before Mark could reach the wheel, Angelique recovered herself and righted them on course. Mark protested her taking the risk, but she yelled over the engine roar, "Let me handle it, I've run boats since I was ten! You have to stop them!"

146

Mark quickly formed a crude plan, based on their maneuver in the lagoon. He went to where Bobby knelt on the deck, grasping the boy with one big hand, bearing down. Pain brought the youngster out of his shock. "Bobby, I need your help. Come with me," Mark commanded. They went to the wheel, where he continued to outline his idea. "Listen close, both of you. Angelique, I want you to run into water as shallow as we can take. Then, Bobby, you crawl out on the bow. You're the smallest and they shouldn't see you from behind us. Take this knife with you," he handed the boy his Buck clasp-knife. "When I give you a signal, throw the anchor over the side. When you feel the anchor grab hold, Angelique, cut power and spin the wheel. As soon as we do a one-eighty, Bobby, and the anchor line comes taut, cut us free from it. Then pour the power on and steer directly back toward the other boat, Angelique, and both of you keep low. Now, let's go."

He turned away from them and crossed to the bunk, picking up the M-79 grenade launcher he had taken from his attaché case and assembled. The Penetrator slung a bandolier of five rounds over his shoulder, dropping four more into a pocket. The weapon looked like a long-barrel flare gun with a shoulder stock and loaded, single shot, the same way. He snapped open the breech and inserted a stubby 40mm round, then turned back to the others.

Bobby Reevé had already complied with his instructions, the Penetrator was pleased to see. The slim youngster lay crouched below the high bow rail, both hands clutching the small anchor. Gaston was sitting up, leaning against the forward cabin wall, his face a pale, sickly greenish hue. He tried to smile encouragement but broke it off in a grimace of pain. Mark stepped past him, out onto the forward

147

deck, bracing himself against the cabin wall. Bullets still snapped past as he watched the waters shoaling. As the water changed from a mud-stained deep blue to yellow-green, he raised one arm.

"Now!" he shouted, dropping his arm. Bobby dropped the anchor. There came a sudden silence as the hook took hold and Angelique throttled back. They began a bobbing, rolling, dizzying swing, gut-wrenchingly close to seasickness, as they turned around, connected to their underwater pivot point by a thin line. A quick look at the Gulfland boat and the Penetrator set his sights for maximum range. His eyes were fixed on his target, the crow's nest from which P.K. was firing, some twenty feet up a stubby mast. The odds against a direct hit at this range, from a boat, were incredible, but he would settle for anything that would keep the sniper's head down.

Mark felt a lurch as Bobby cut the line; then he was pressed backward as engines surged to full open. Less than five seconds had passed, leaving the Gulfland crew no time to discover their tactics. The Penetrator loosed his first round as soon as he balanced himself against the acceleration. It fell short and twenty yards wide of the target, detonating when it struck the surface. They were still too far apart to read expressions, but reactions aboard the *Ibis* were easy to guess. Few, if any of them, Mark knew, would have bargained for this. Thugs accustomed to terrorizing virtually unarmed fishermen and their families would hardly be prepared for the realities of war. His second shot fell close alongside, near the bow, razor-sharp steel fragments chopping wood from the hull.

Their range was constantly closing, yet it was luck as much as accuracy that placed his third round close to the target, hitting a cross arm to one side and below the crow's nest. The effect was similar to that in 'Nam when the troops put one into a tree to get a sniper. The defoliating action of whizzing steel shards chewed up part of the bottom and side of the plywood bucket. Peter Keoh stood part way out of the crow's nest, his mouth twisted in an unheard howl of agony. His rifle slipped over the combing, falling into the bay. With the sniper disarmed, Mark concentrated on a bigger target.

Three fast rounds into the base of the short mast, where it connected to the cabin roof, and it was tottering drunkenly, weaving in the vicious cross chop they were forced to breast. The mast gave a final lurch and toppled over the side, spilling P.K. into the water. He surfaced quickly and began to flounder toward the boat. Then the water around him churned up in miniature geysers. Peter Keoh threw up his arms, frothy blood bubbling from his mouth, and sank below the surface.

Engine noise had prevented the Penetrator from hearing the shots and his attention had been entirely on the action. Now he looked down at the bow of the *Christy Sue*. Bobby Reevé was kneeling at the rail, reloading his father's Ruger carbine.

"That was for Uncle Jiggs," he shouted gleefully as he directed his fire at the cabin of the other boat. They were less than fifty yards apart as the Penetrator joined in, putting a round on the forward deck as Phil DuBois loosed another burst from his M-2 carbine. Bouchet's number two man rose to his full height, screaming his way into hell as the thin slivers of steel chewed his back into a pulp. His screams cut off as .22 slugs stitched up his chest. Mark's next shot went through the forward cabin port and the Gulfland boat, *Ibis*, slewed off to one side.

Mark signaled Angelique to cut the engines and they drifted toward the target. There was no sign of the *Ibis* crew continuing the fight, but the Penetrator made sure. His last two mini-grenades went into the cabin. There was a soft whump as the gas tanks went, then the cabin was hidden in a ball of orange flame. They watched it in fascination for a moment, then made course for Grand Isle.

Behind the *Christy Sue*, the *Ibis* continued to burn until it was a drifting, lifeless hulk, gutted to the water line.

Chapter 15

INTERCEPTION PLAY

Early Tuesday morning, Mark located the photographer. John Carpenter readily agreed to accompany Angelique to Baton Rouge to contact the Secret Service counterfeiting detail and the Attorney General's office.

Angelique protested that with the photographer's testimony there was no reason for her to go, that she should stay in New Orleans until it was over. Mark firmly refused and saw her packed into Carpenter's car along with the evidence and on their way.

On the previous evening, after their return to Grand Isle, Gaston Reevé had been treated by their family doctor. At their insistence, and for a hundred-dollar bill, the doctor agreed to withhold from the police the mandatory gunshot report until Wednesday. The bullet had torn through the muscle below Gaston's left shoulder blade—a clean hole—and turned outward, punching another neat hole between his biceps and the bone. A fraction of an inch more and it would have ripped his arm off. He was stiff and very sore, but otherwise able to get around.

Their biggest problem had been finding a way to take care of Jiggs' body. Mark had suggested burial at sea, in light of the situation. Gaston protested that there were many who would want to attend the funeral. Jiggs deserved, he insisted, proper mourning and a church funeral. With considerable misgivings, Mark agreed to bring the body ashore and find a place for him. Their search took them to a Negro funeral parlor. There, more hundred-dollar bills from Mark's money belt bought silence.

At the funeral home, grief—and the realization that he had killed a man—caught up to Bobby Reevé. His body trembled and huge tears wet his anguished face as he threw himself against his father, tormented sobs shaking his slender frame. Gaston held Bobby in his arms, tears of pain and grief on his own cheeks, and soothed the boy. He agreed to allow his son to stay at the mortuary, keeping a vigil until time for the funeral.

Now, under an overcast mid-day sky, Gaston asked Mark a vexing question. "How are we to find this rendezvous point?"

It was a problem the Penetrator had given much consideration since their return. He thought aloud, forming an idea as he spoke. "All we know for sure is that they are going to pick up the counterfeit tonight, out beyond territorial waters. And the name of the ship they'll use, *La Belle de Mer*. It's certain they will leave from the Gulfland dock. But when and what waterways they'll use is anybody's guess."

"We can always tie up on the west bank and watch for *La Belle* to shove off," Gaston suggested.

"And tail them from there. Good idea. Let's take the *Christy Sue* upriver now." Mark loaded considerable equipment for their expedition and, in half an hour, they were ready.

Gaston took a short cut, up Barataria Bay to the Innercoastal Waterway and on to the Harvey Canal. It brought them out into the Mississippi seventeen blocks above Gulfland. Just under two hours after they left Grand Isle, they were tied up at a public

152

dock off First and Lafayette in Gretna, within sight of *La Belle de Mer*. Gaston purchased a fixture and lens from the ship fitter's store and replaced his starboard running light. With Mark's suggestion and money, he bought another complete set of lights and a handful of toggle switches. As the afternoon wore down to evening, they installed them in such a way that a switch could put out a single light or by using several switches, any combination. Also, by throwing the proper switches, to an observer, the port side became starboard, starboard port.

Mardi Gras was nearly over and the Maskers Ball only three hours off when *La Belle de Mer* cast off and got underway. She ran sedately up the main channel, past their position, turning south into the Harvey Canal. They left the dock with Mark handling the wheel while Gaston tended the engines and fuel supply.

They ran into the Gulf of Mexico with the swollen red sun setting off their starboard beam. As the afterglow of twilight faded into darkness, Mark switched on the running lights. He asked Gaston to keep record of their compass bearings. "Let me know if they start zig-zagging, give any sign they think we're following."

Three quarters of an hour passed, with Gaston checking the compass every five minutes, before he touched Mark's shoulder. "They're on to us," Gaston told Mark. Holding up a chart in the greenish cabin light, he ticked off the points. "Here to here to here in the last fifteen minutes. We're not halfway to international waters and we ought to be out already." Mark cut all running lights, except the masthead white and starboard green.

"Let them think we turned off," he said. They ran that way for five minutes, then, when they were again

153

in the trough of a wave, he reversed the running lights and lit a white light on the bow. Aboard *La Belle de Mer*, it would now look as if they were moving in the opposite direction, back toward land, or perhaps lying dead in the water. They continued like that for another quarter hour, heading due south, falling off a little to port to help the illusion.

"We're getting close to the limit line," Gaston informed Mark. The Penetrator nodded to acknowledge the report and the next time they dropped out of sight of the *Belle*, he cut all lights, increasing the throttles to full. Gaston took the wheel and the Penetrator moved to the bunk where his combat gear was laid out. He was going full bore for this operation. In addition to the M-79, with tear-gas rounds added to its ammo, he had brought along his sweet little Secret Service model Uzi, complete with full-barrel silencer. The surprise effect of the silent SMG would be an added psychological advantage. He dumped half-a-dozen M-3 fraggers into a purselike satchel he slung over one shoulder, counterbalanced by six fifty-round mags of 9mm parabellums for the Uzi fitted into a cloth bandolier on the other. The Israeli squirt gun hung free, between his arms, on a nylon cord. The grenade launcher, with its musette bag of ammunition and a gas mask completed his equipment. He lugged it all onto the forward deck, passing Gaston, who revved his engines higher, cutting through the water toward the distant boat.

Tackling *La Belle de Mer* was a major enterprise, requiring split-hair timing and all the cunning of a jungle beast. She was a hundred-ton purse seiner, of all-steel construction, built on the West coast at *San Diego Marine Construction* as a tuna boat. She carried a crew of fifteen, plus officers and who-knew-how-many gunmen tonight. The broad, low fantail, sloping to the water line seemed her only vulnerable point. It was decided that here was where the Penetrator—a one-man boarding party—would change ships and hopefully capture the enemy vessel. They were running up to the port side now and the Penetrator slipped his gas mask in place, loading the M-79.

Working as fast as he could to chamber new rounds, the Penetrator dumped four tear-gas shells along the port side, the last one into the pilot house. They rounded the bow, cutting speed, and he unloosed six more. He was picking up scattered return fire from a few handguns, but none connected with the *Christy Sue*. Then they were at the stern. Mark laid down the grenade launcher. He had shown Gaston how to fire it, in case he was forced to retreat and needed covering fire. It would be handy there in case of such an eventuality. Backing and filling, Captain Reevé maneuvered his small shrimp boat into position beside the huge steel fantail. As *La Belle de Mer* began to rise on the swell of the next wave and *Christy Sue* dipped, they came level. Gaston gave a final snort on the engines as the Penetrator poised a second . . . and leaped across.

What the hell are those idiots shooting at? Carlo Santini had been enjoying his leader's prerogative, taking a nap before *La Belle de Mer* rendezvoused with the Cuban ship.

Bunch o' goddamned amateurs. That's been the trouble with this deal all along. Too many fuckin' amateurs. No real leadership. Colbert and DuBois! They couldn't find their way to the toilet, let alone *lead* anyone. P.K. wasn't bad, as long as he had stuck to what he did best. But he was just a two-bit gunsel. Even Bouchet's into something too big for him. Shoulda' done like Uncle Vito said, gone into Our Thing. Shit! Ten years a cop and nothin' to show for it. But this is it. *The* big score. After this, you name it. Start your own Family, or maybe South America. With all that dough in gold a guy could take over one'a them banana republics and be president for life.

Got to get it first. That means stop them dummys from shootin'. Bouchet said the Cubans were real nervous about bein' so close to the States. Scare the spics off and no score for anybody . . . Santini shrugged into his underslung shoulder rig, put the big .357 into it, and headed for the door.

"Christ!" he shouted aloud, staggering back into the stateroom. "Tear gas! What the fuck is this?" He wet a small towel in the wash basin, covering his nose and mouth, and ventured out into the companionway. Moving fast, he was in the pilot house a few seconds later.

More gas filled the air. All ports were open and exhaust fans labored to clear the fumes out, but made little progress. Everyone was gasping and choking from the effects of the chemical agent and the boat had come to a standstill. Carlo Santini herded them out on deck. A stiff sea breeze blew away the effects of the gas. "What happened?" he demanded of Captain Girrard.

"A boat ran in on us without lights," the captain of *La Belle de Mer* told him. "Next thing we knew the place was full of tear gas. Got a report somebody boarded us at the fantail."

"We'll take care of that sonofabitch," Santini declared. He sent a seaman below to his cabin to get the harbor police's only Thompson. It had to be this Penetrator bastard. No matter how many he'd got before, it was gonna be different now. Show that son

156

of a bitch. Those other guys had been amateurs. The Penetrator was up against a pro this time.

There was a muffled *whump* and the deck plates beneath Santini's feet lurched, something rattling against their undersides like hail. Thirty seconds later it was repeated on the other side. What the hell was that... ?

Gumsoled shoes bit into spray-slicked steel. The hold slipped, started to give. Leaning far forward, legs churning to get purchase, the Penetrator labored up the steep ramp.

He made the top! Mark Hardin stood between two piles of net, swaying with the motion of the boat, getting his bearings. Two dark forms rushed onto the rear deck from a darker companionway. Up came the Uzi. Squeeze gently and get off it. Both men sprawled bonelessly to the deck before either one could fire a shot. They were still twitching when the Penetrator got in motion, heading for the same dark hatchway they had come from. Two down, how many more?

To one side, two other men popped up from behind a pile of net. One of them swung a shotgun into line. The shotgun discharged high into the air as a swarm of silent parabellums whispered their death song. The burst flipped both men backward, overboard, into the sea. Four down, more to come. . . .

Yellow-orange eyes winked at the Penetrator from down the dark companionway. He pressed himself to one side, hand dipping into the musette bag. The pin came free and he slipped the spoon, tossing the grenade into the dark opening. It detonated with an ear-ringing *whang* off the steel walls. He crossed to the starboard companionway and bounced another fragger along the cork-stripped deck plates.

BA-WHANG!

"Hey, man. We give up! Ya hear me? No more We give," a voice called from the darkness.

Problems. What do you do with prisoners in the middle of a DA strike? Not even time to search them. The Penetrator pulled up his gas mask. "Get in the cabins. Lock the doors and stay there," he ordered. Isolate them and mop up afterward. They could be crew members. He stepped through the hatchway. . . .

Three men were still outside the cabins. They all held guns. *Pfis-zirr-zirr-zirr!* The Uzi spoke again. Three more deaders. The Penetrator picked his way through the bodies. A muffled voice came from behind one door.

"Hey mister, they made us do it."

"Don't take it out on us," another voice called. "It's not our fight."

"Yeah," came a third, "we only work here."

Crew members. The information was filed for reference. It would make things easier later. Stairway ahead. It must lead to the upper deck and pilot house.

Carlo Santini had his Thompson.

Funny how that big mother made a guy feel better just to hold it. This Penetrator might be a one-man army, but trust this sweet old chopper to bring him down to size. Jeez! Where's a guy get all that shit? Tear gas? Grenades? A submachine gun, yeah, but *silenced?* Christ, all you could hear was them ricochets zinging down the companionway, but no gun firing. Silencer or no, he tries to get up here he'll get his smart ass tommygunned right in two. Get out on deck, that's the place to get him. Take that fuck-head captain along, too. He's got as big a stake in this as anyone.

Christ! There he is. He looks like a man from Mars, long snout, big, glassy eyes. Gas mask, that's all it is. The Thompson chuckled its steady rhythm in Santini's hands. The face was gone now, down below deck level. He was on the run!

Clank!

What was that? Mother of God! A gren . . .

Just before he died—his belly ripped open by grenade fragments, guts spilled on the deck—Paul Girrard, captain of *La Belle de Mer*, looked over at Carlo Santini. "The money. Was all that money worth . . . this?" he asked.

Santini didn't answer the question. He had a leg blown off, his life running out of him into a sticky red pool at the severed end. He was too busy to answer, trying to remember that thing he used to say as a kid. How did it go? . . . *pray for us sinners now, and at the hour of our . . .*

Mark Hardin flicked the afterdeck work lights—their prearranged signal. The battle was over.

By the time he reached the fantail, Gaston had maneuvered *Christy Sue* into position at the ramp. He threw a line across and the Penetrator started up the slippery incline. As he made the line fast at the winch, two crewmen appeared in a hatchway.

"Hey, buddy. We'll give you a hand. You're doin' it all wrong." Problem solved.

After winching the *Christy Sue* aboard and securing her behind the net skiff, Mark and Gaston had a talk with the crew members. None of them had known what their captain and chief were getting them into. When they were told about the phony money and the effect it would have on the country, they agreed to run the boat and do anything they could to help.

159

They dumped the corpses over the side and go underway. One crewman came to Mark. When the Gulfland hard guys came aboard with Santini, he told the Penetrator, they brought some funny-looking boxes and a heavy package wrapped in a tarp. He took the Penetrator down to the cabin where they had stored the things.

When Mark saw the three-and-a-half-foot wooden crates and the long metal tube resting in its wrappings, a smile creased his lips. "Get that stuff up to the pilot house," he ordered. "We might need it later."

Gaston located a chart, with the rendezvous point clearly marked. He steered a course directly there. As they neared the spot, the sleek lines of a Royal Canadian Navy-type corvette stood out against the light horizon. A signal lamp flickered and Gaston consulted a signals list attached to the captain's orders. They made the proper reply and were called along side. Lines were hove and they tied up.

"¡Hola! Camaradas! Which one of you is Señor Santini, the man in charge for the dinero?"

"¡Soy yo!" Mark called across. "Carlo Santini."

As he walked to the rail, crewmen came on deck, a winch whined, and the hatch cover to a forward fishwell opened. Through the glare of a tight beam spotlight that illuminated the pilot house and deck, the Penetrator noticed that as crewmen worked at the fishwell, Cuban soldiers came to the rail of the corvette. Each of them held a short-barreled submachinegun.

"What ship is that?" asked the Cuban interrogator.

"La Belle de Mer," Mark said. "You received a radio message about the change?" That was obvious,

160

or the Cuban officer would never have known San-
ini's name.

"*Si.*" A jury-rigged cargo boom rattled aboard the
Cuban vessel, drawing a loaded forklift pad from
the bowels of the ship. It swung overside and lowered its burden into the open hatch on the deck below the Penetrator.

"It is not so good to be so close to *Los Estados
Unidos.* My men, they worry. They go to work too
fast, no? I have forgot to ask the all-important question, *verdad?* Señor Santini, I would have the name
of your mother, *por favor.*"

A verifying password. The Penetrator had expected such, had memorized the five alternative pass-
words listed in the instructions, but this was not
among them. Would they really know Santini's
mother's name? Could he fake it? "Maria Angelica,"
he answered smoothly.

"*¡Estamos chasgueados!*" the Cuban yelled, grabbing for his pistol. "*¡Este hombre no es del Señor
Bouchet!*" His words were carried with him into
oblivion as the Penetrator blasted out the center of
the Cuban's chest with flat-nosed .45 slugs.

At the same instant, several Cuban soldiers
opened fire on the Penetrator with their submachine
guns.

Chapter 16

A SMALL ACT OF PIRACY

Mark dashed for the open pilot house door, jack-eted slugs bouncing off the steel deck to both sides, as the Cuban soldiers continued to pour it on with their burp guns.

One of the crewmen, thinking fast, cut the boom rope, dropping part of the money shipment into their hold. Then he scurried to cover. Gaston hit the throttle arm, actuating the engine-room telegraph, and swung the wheel, nosing them away from the corvette. The bow line parted with a sharp report and they slowly began to make way. An entire window blew away in the rear of the pilot house and he cursed softly, urging more speed out of *La Belle de Mer.*

Mark scooped up the Uzi and emptied the remaining magazines onto the Cubans' deck. Two soldiers were hit and the others dived for cover. On the corvette's forward deck, a guncrew manned the 40mm twin-mount. The trainer was still cranking the gun around when they burned off the first two clips, shells bursting in a wide arc, coming nowhere near *La Belle.*

Exchanging his Uzi for the M-79, the Penetrator concentrated on silencing this deadly opposition. His first shot fell short, striking the high bow plates. The next round went off on the forward deck, cutting an ammo bearer's legs out from under him, sending a banana clip of 40mm ammunition skittering across the deck. His third round was right on target, killing or wounding the entire guncrew. Their brief respite was a mixed blessing. They gained speed with each second, but distance likewise, drawing them out of effective small-arms range. Mark fired another grenade, only to see it fall far short of the corvette. Worse yet, another crew was manning the forties, cranking the twin barrels closer onto target. Those babies had a range over two thousand yards and fired AP rounds and incendiaries as well as HE and tracer. Maximum speed for a boat like *La Belle de Mer* was fourteen to eighteen knots, which would keep them under the guns far too long.

As forty-millimeter shells burst, first to port, then starboard, the Penetrator lugged the wooden crates and tarp-wrapped bundle out of the pilot house onto the after-pilot deck. The crewman who had cut the boom line helped him. Then they unwrapped the tarp, revealing an obsolete 75mm recoilless rifle. "You ever serve one of these things?" Mark asked the young fisherman. He received a negative shake of the head as the crewman stared in fascination at the sharply tapered, wicked-looking tube. "You'll do. Now watch this closely."

Mark showed him how to turn the locking handles and open the breech. Then the Penetrator took a graceful-looking round with its ventilated casing from one wooden crate and chambered it. He closed the breech and shouldered the weapon. "When you have it locked securely," he instructed, "get well clear of the relief ports and tap me on the head."

Mark felt the other man's tap as he pressed his face to the rubber eyepiece of the sight. The corvette snapped into view, a black silhouette against a

163

green field. Range marks glowed a luminous yellow-green in vertical increments. Despite the shells screeching around them, the Penetrator aimed for the largest part of his target. The world turned yellow-white as flame billowed from the relief ports, with force equal to the forward discharge of the projectile, reflected in wavering brightness from the white-painted outside of the pilot house. A couple of seconds later they were rewarded by a flash and explosion in the superstructure of the Cuban vessel. The Korean War vintage snorter shot a little high, the Penetrator noted, before rapidly firing three more rounds, blowing away the bridge and radio shack. Then he lined up on the guns.

Craaack-ack-ack! A guitar-string vibration thrummed through the boat as a long burst of 40mm shells smashed into *La Belle de Mer*. Gaston called to him and Mark hurried inside the pilot house. A damage report was coming up from the engineering space. "We got holed ten-twelve places below the water line. We're shippin' a hell of a lot of water. Couple of guys dead down here and the auxiliary generator's out. We can't use the bilge pumps. We'll have to go to manual operation." The acting chief's words received ominous emphasis as the boat lurched, seeming to settle in the water, slowing down.

"Can we switch over to main generator?" Gaston asked.

"Sure, but it'll take time, which we don't got."

"You handle that, Avery. We'll go to manual until you get it rigged. Have all hands man the pumps." The boat's sideward jerks were more pronounced now as several tons of unbaffled water sloshed around below decks. Another burst from the Cubans ripped through the staterooms one deck down and Mark headed for the recoilless.

164

With his assistant gunner on pump detail, the Penetrator had to load for himself. It was a tricky operation, slow and awkward. Considerable delay came between shots. The 40s kept up a constant hail of explosive shells while he traded shots. Their exchange developed into a gun duel unlike anything since the German raider *Atlantis* was sunk in 1944. The rapid-fire Cuban guns poured hundreds of rounds into the purse seiner before Mark landed two solid hits on the gun mount, silencing it forever. He had only two rounds left.

It was time to pay them back in kind. The Penetrator put the last two 75s into the corvette, just below the waterline, amidships. Flame poured from after hatchways and the ship began to list to starboard. The Cubans were trapped.

Their guns were useless, a great hole gaped in the hull, the Penetrator's earlier shelling had blown away their lifeboats, and fires raged below decks. With their radio room and controls shot away, they sat helpless in the water, unable to move or call for assistance.

To fire on any nation's ship in international waters was an act of piracy, but the Penetrator was little concerned by that fact. They had on board only ten or so of the eighty million in counterfeit the Cuban had told him about. Mark estimated that the Cuban sailors would be too busy fighting fires to deal with the remainder before they were apprehended by the Coast Guard. Provided, of course, that Angelique and John Carpenter had convinced the Secret Service of the urgency of the situation and they had acted in time. Mark threw the recoilless rifle and ammunition boxes over the side and joined Gaston.

Inside the pilot house, the lights dimmed and brightened, then dimmed again. "Son-of-a-gun!"

Gaston exclaimed joyfully. "He got the pumps hooked on the main. We'll make it now, *mon ami*." Mark switched on the radio, tuning to the Coast Guard frequency. Only a few minutes passed before they were able to verify that a cutter was on its way to investigate a report of "gunfire at sea." They cut all running lights and set course for Grand Isle. The problem of the counterfeit money was out of the way.

But there still remained Marcel Bouchet.

Chapter 17

J'ACCUSE

Marcel Bouchet felt the pressure growing.

All hell had exploded around him and he was fighting with all he had to keep control of his empire. How could one man do it? How was it possible that this Penetrator bastard could be in town only four days and his whole organization wiped out? The money, at least, was safe aboard *La Belle de Mer*. It would be in later in the day.

Funny that Santini hadn't radioed in. But maybe it was better this way. If only he didn't have to hold this meeting now. But it still took at least the appearance of an election to put Co-op officials in office, and he needed to get his trusted replacements in before the money was distributed. God-double-damn the Penetrator! If it hadn't been for him, nothing would have gone wrong. No time for that now. Better get on with it.

Auditorium B, on the main floor of Gulfland's office building, was filled with tired but noisy fishermen. They paid little attention to the preliminaries being conducted by the secretary, laughing and talking with friends while the routine business of the meeting proceded on the stage before them. The air was blue with cigar and pipe smoke. From time to time, they interrupted their nonstop conversations long enough to shout an "Aye," although completely ignorant of the nature or content of the motions they approved. Silence rippled across the membership, however, as Marcel Bouchet took the speaker's rostrum.

"Gentlemen. Brothers. The first order of new business is the election of new officers," Bouchet's voice dropped, assuming a mournful tone, edged with righteous anger, "to fill the vacancies created by the violent and unnecessary deaths of Brother Colbert and Brother Dubois." Bouchet was about to call for nominations when his words dried up, his mouth hanging open. The wide double doors at the rear of the auditorium were thrown wide and Angelique Rubidaux entered. Every head turned to watch her walk down the aisle.

She clutched a large sheaf of papers to her breast and walked with purposeful, controlled presence to the floor mike, set below the stage apron. Her outward calm, however, did not reflect the nervousness gnawing at her mind. . . .

When the Penetrator and Gaston returned, she had told them that the Secret Service agents were laying plans with the police for their raid on Gulfland. They had said it would take several hours to get search warrants and a warrant for Bouchet's arrest for murder and counterfeiting. When the Coast Guard reported seizing the Cuban corvette, all shot up and surrounded by floating packets of counterfeit money, they said it would delay them further—they would want to inventory the bogus cash and interrogate the survivors. Yet another delay was predicted by the Secret Service when Angelique reported to them that *La Belle de Mer* was tied up in Grand Isle with more of the counterfeit aboard.

It was a certain fact, the three of them agreed,

that Bouchet would soon realize that something had gone wrong. All of the time wasted in completing the legal formalities and paper work would allow him to escape. Mark left to make preparations to continue a direct action solution, to finish Bouchet himself. Gaston, exhausted by a night of heavy action and the effects of his wound, opted for sleep. Left on her own, Angelique came up with the idea of taking the whole thing to the Co-op members. Something had to be done to stop Bouchet. There was a sunrise meeting to elect new officers. Surely, if they knew the truth, they would do something to prevent Bouchet's escape until the Secret Service arrested him. . . .

Her voice was firm and clear as she spoke into the mike. "Mr. President, I request the floor to read an announcement of greatest importance to the entire membership."

Marcel Bouchet's smug confidence crumbled into panic. My God! Those papers. She has what the old man hid. It's that goddamned Penetrator! Because of him everything is lost. Have to stall her. Get away and radio Santini to land the money somewhere else. They'll not get it or me. A guy can live a long time on eighty million in one of the countries that won't extradite you. Easy to pass it, too, and no way to prove it's phony. Play for time. What to do? Stall, drag it out. "I'm sorry, but your request is out of order at this time, Miss Rubidaux," he answered her, his voice barely under control.

"For the sake of my father's memory," Angelique said, directing her appeal to the members, "I beg you, let me read this. It's so very important to you all."

"Out of order! Out of order!" Bouchet shouted, his

panic breaking through. "Leave the mike! We have business to do."

"Let her talk," one fisherman called.

"There's no motion on the floor," another added.

Another fisherman, one Angelique recognized as a close friend of her father, was at her side at the mike. "Point of ... what the shit is it? ... Point of personal privilege."

"She's not a member," Bouchet countered.

"That don't matter, let us hear her!" demanded several men.

Bouchet tried to block them again, "But ..."

"Mais on s'en faut comme d'une musette!" rumbled a bass voice, in Cajun French, from the center of the auditorium. *"But we don't give a damn!* Let her say what she wants."

This was getting out of hand. His stalling had backfired, gone on too long. No matter what she had to say there was no real proof without the money. There's a chance to get away while she's talking. No cops, nothing to worry about. Let her keep them busy.

"All right! All right! Quiet down," Bouchet demanded, using more time to think. "She's not a member and it's against the rules to let her speak." Angry voices rose again. "Wait a minute! If you want to hear her, we have to pass a motion to suspend the rules. Do I hear such a motion?"

"So move," boomed the man beside Angelique.

"Second?" The auditorium roared with sound. "Those in favor?" Another roar. "Opposed?"

"Fuck you, Bouchet!" an anonymous fisherman yelled. It was getting worse than he thought.

"Miss Rubidaux, the floor is yours. Would you like to come up here?" A scattering of applause accompanied his gesture.

170

Angelique stood at the podium, her papers spread before her. What could she say? She hadn't expected to get the chance to speak so easily. She took a deep breath, glancing nervously at Marcel Bouchet, who stood a short way behind her, to the right.

"Gulf fishermen. Those of you who were friends of my father. All of you. Listen to me. Some of you won't believe what I am going to say, but it's true. Every bit of it." She looked so small and vulnerable behind the large lectern. Her face was pale with tension, emphasized by her long black hair. Her dark eyes were fearful yet defiant. She raised some of the papers in one hand. "I have the proof right here. Marcel Bouchet is using you. He's using Gulfland Co-op as a front for a monstrous scheme. He's had my father murdered and his men have tried to kill me."

Time to get out while there was still a chance. Marcel Bouchet started walking casually toward the wings, headed for an escape route that would take him through his office and to the extra cash he had there in his safe. Shouts of anger came from the fishermen. First he had to shut up this girl. Stop her before she could say too much.

"He's working with the Communists in Cuba, to bring in counterfeit money. Lots of it. Enough to bankrupt our country . . . and he's using the co-op to hide what he's doing."

More angry shouts and several men left their seats. Bouchet hurried between the red velvet curtain legs, off stage. He crossed to where the amplifier sat on a table, its operator seated behind, bending over it. "Harry, cut that goddamned broad off," he demanded.

"Can't," the PA man replied.

Bouchet was about to snap a sharp reprimand at

the noncompliant employee, when he discovered the reason Harry refused. Marcel Bouchet looked up into the thick, ugly snout of a silencer.

Behind the massive .45 caliber death machine, held in his right fist, the Penetrator shook his head. "She's going to tell it all, Bouchet." On stage, Angelique was reading from a photocopy of her father's note, holding up copies of the enlargements John Carpenter had made. Angry voices shouted from the audience. A growing mutter of discontent rumbled under these outbursts.

Bouchet was defeated and he knew it. Only his fear compelled him on. Jesus, this guy was big, he thought as he eyed the extension barrel and silencer on the Penetrator's Colt Commander. A rig like that costs money. There has to be some way to get to a guy like this. "I have money," he said. "Enough for both of us. Sinking the *Jenté Alouette* got you into trouble with the law. And killing all my men that day. You don't have any more chance than I do. Come with me. Together we can beat them all."

"Not a chance." The Penetrator centered his .45 on Bouchet's chest, then continued, "I told you I could kill you any time I wanted to. Now seems as good a time as any." But his words were drowned out by a mob roar. Angelique's revelations had created a monster. Men surged from their seats, enraged by what they had heard. They charged toward the stage, determined to seek out Marcel Bouchet, with lynch law on their minds.

Despite his slight build and deceptive effeminate gestures, when it was necessary, Marcel Bouchet could act swiftly, with considerable strength. As the Penetrator was briefly distracted by the raging mob heading their way, Bouchet upset the table, dumping audio equipment and its operator onto his

172

captor. Mark Hardin went sprawling in a tangle of cables, arms, and legs. He pulled himself free in time to see Bouchet's feet and legs disappear off a steel ladder onto the fly gallery. Daylight momentarily flooded the upper reaches of the stage and a red light automatically began to blink. A fire exit, leading to the second floor! The Penetrator started in pursuit of his fleeing quarry as the mob stormed backstage. He was inundated by angry fishermen as they dashed around, seeking the missing Gulfland president. Unnoticed in the darkened area, he made his way unobtrusively to the ladder and started up. Just as the Penetrator stepped onto the fly floor, someone located the work light switch and flooded the backstage space with brightness. With a roar of triumph, they began their search anew.

In the hallway beyond the fire door, the Penetrator considered Bouchet's probable route of escape. He had mentioned money; the obvious place would be his third-floor office. He reached the top floor in time to see Bouchet disappear down the rear stairwell. Holstering his .45 in order to make better time, he ran to the stairs. Bouchet's footsteps made clattering echoes up the concrete shaft. The Penetrator took loping strides downward, skipping steps and jumping to landings, closing with the man ahead of him. He came within sight of Bouchet, then jerked to a stop as a small-caliber bullet ricocheted off the concrete walls, passing close to his head with a whining screech. It was followed by the pop of a tiny weapon Mark estimated to be a .25 auto. A door slammed and he surged forward again.

Bouchet was halfway to the processing plant when the Penetrator came out of the office building. In the open now, he tried a couple of shots, missing

173

both times at that range. The Penetrator answered in kind. Big .45 slugs smacking into the asphalt added impetus to Bouchet's dash for freedom. Reaching his goal, he threw open a door and ran into the plant.

Mark approached the door cautiously, now that he knew his enemy was armed. He stepped to one side and opened the door, pulling it toward him. Three shots came in a rapid terrier snarl. Two slugs hit the door, stinging his left hand with their impact. He pulled it all the way open, securing the door in its wall catch. He held the silenced Commander in his big hand again, crouching to dive through the opening.

Marcel Bouchet sobbed with desperation. He knew now that he had trapped himself. The only way out was the door and that way lay the Penetrator and death. He could go out one of the big cargo doors, but it was slow work throwing the bolts and drawing one of them up by its chain. The Penetrator could take all the time he wanted, standing in the open, to fire bullet after bullet. A shudder passed through his body, as if feeling the impact of each slug.

He could always go up. The galleries lead to the storage area behind the processing floor with its tangle of cookers and canning equipment. It would have to be that. It was his only choice.

A sudden blur of motion brought his attention back to the doorway. A dark form filled it for a second and the little Astra .25 that he had hurriedly reloaded yammered again. Six times. An almost feminine cry of frustration escaped Bouchet as he realized he had emptied the pistol. Sweat popped out on his face as he released the magazine catch, dropping the tiny metal box into his left hand. Laying the pistol in his lap, he groped in a side pocket for loose shells. His hands shook uncontrollably as he struggled to fit cartridges into the magazine. They dribbled from his hand, clattering against the plastic tiled floor. Sobbing in terror, he shoved the partly-loaded magazine into the Astra and fired wildly at an unseen target. When it clicked on empty, he threw the small weapon toward the door. A frightful keening escaped his lips as he dashed for the ladder that led to the gallery, clutching tightly the bag that contained the stacks of bills he had taken from his safe.

Bouchet's shots sent the Penetrator down, hugging the floor until he heard the pistol clattering against metal legs to one side. Then he was up in a kneeling position, his .45 ready. He had only a second to orient himself before he saw a flash of movement between pieces of machinery. A glance told him where Bouchet must be heading and he was ready for him. He let his target get nearly to the top of the ladder before standing and lining up his sights. It was a target range exercise. Let out half a breath, hold it . . .

Thock! Thock! The shots sounded like a man's finger striking a wooden box. But the bullets hit low. One cut through Bouchet's lower abdomen, while the other smashed his hips. He was shoved forward into the ladder as a grunt of pain was forced from his lips. The grunt turned to a scream of horror that echoed through the processing room, as involuntary reaction pushed him backward and he fell away.

Bouchet's scream was cut off as he landed in a huge cauldron of boiling shrimp soup. He surfaced slowly, shrieking in agony as the flesh cooked from

175

his bones. Still clutching his bag of money, his twisted mouth emitting inhuman cries, Marcel Bouchet sank below the pinkish, shrimp-flecked surface for the final time.

EPILOGUE

High above the Mississippi River's muddy ribbon, Mark Hardin trimmed the Baron B-58 and set course into the sun toward California and the Stronghold.

Curiosity sent his hand to the radio and he cranked it over to the standard broadcast band.

"Early this morning a joint announcement was made by the Secret Service and the United States Coast Guard that rocked the entire nation," the announcer's excited voice began. "Their statement, released in New Orleans at nine thirty-five Eastern Daylight Time indicated that at three A.M. today, the Coast Guard cutter *Admiral Bird* had seized a Cuban naval corvette off the coast of Louisiana. On board they found nearly seventy million dollars in counterfeit United States currency. Reliable sources in New Orleans indicated that the phony money was so perfect that it could not be distinguished from the real thing. When questioned on this point, Treasury officials refused comment.

"Meanwhile, in Washington," the commentator went on, "the President announced that he would send a stern note of protest to Havana, demanding that adequate guarantees be given by the Castro government to insure that there would be no similar incidents in the future.

"Back with news on the local scene, including the alleged connection between prominent fishing co-op magnate Marcel Bouchet and the counterfeit scheme after this important announcement . . ."

"Be more likely to get cooperation," the Penetrator grumbled, "if they delivered that note in Castro's lap, wrapped around the nose of a thousand-pound bomb."

It was all over now. Nothing left but useless noises and meaningless ritual played out by the politicians. The real threat, the possibility of economic disaster, was as dead as Marcel Bouchet.

Mardi Gras was over too . . . and with it, the massacre brought to town by the Penetrator.

Bouchet had been right, though. Bombing the *Jenté Alouette* had brought the Feds down with a vengeance. The Penetrator was their latest candidate for the Ten Most Wanted list. Maybe it was time to cool it a while. Go to ground and let things settle. Still, there was the pockmarked gunman who had come after him. Who had sent him? Why? Those were questions that needed answering in the near future.

Right now, though, something else was more important. With the Feds jumping around, nervous as an old man in a cat house, it might be a good time to get in that R and R he'd been planning. Perhaps a long stay in the Orient, or South America. Maybe Australia. Somewhere, at least, where the Penetrator was not known and Mark Hardin could relax, forget the wars . . . and be himself.

Violence is a man!
His name is
Edge...

The bloodiest action-series ever published, with a hero who is the meanest, most vicious killer the West has ever seen.

It's sharp —
It's hard —
It's EDGE

GEORGE G. GILMAN

Order	#	Title	Book No.	Price
_____	# 1	The Loner	P109	95¢
_____	# 2	Ten Grand	P115	95¢
_____	# 3	Apache Death	P133	95¢
_____	# 4	Killer's Breed	P148	95¢
_____	# 5	Blood on Silver	P172	95¢
_____	# 6	Red River	P190	95¢
_____	# 7	California Kill	P221	95¢
_____	# 8	Hell's Seven	P265	95¢
_____	# 9	Bloody Summer	P293	95¢
_____	#10	Black Vengeance	P333	95¢

and more to come . . .

TO ORDER
Please check the space next to the book/s you want, send this order form together with your check or money order, include the price of the book/s and 25¢ for handling and mailing, to:

**PINNACLE BOOKS, INC. / P.O. Box 4347
Grand Central Station / New York, N.Y. 10017**
☐ Check here if you want a free catalog.

I have enclosed $_____check_____or money order_____
as payment in full. No C.O.D.'s.

Name_____

Address_____

City_____State_____Zip_____

(Please allow time for delivery)